SHAMEN

BOOK THREE

WRITTEN BY

J.SILVERSTONE

NEYTIRI
PRESS

Published by NEYTIRI PRESS

www.NeytiriPress.com

Cover photo Subbotina Anna, Krakenimages/ shutterstock.com

Printed in the United States of America.

ISBN: 978-1-7352987-3-3

Shamen is a work of fiction. Names, characters, places, and incidents either are the product of the author's imagination or are used fictitiously, and any resemblance to actual persons, living or dead, business establishments, events, or locales is entirely coincidental.

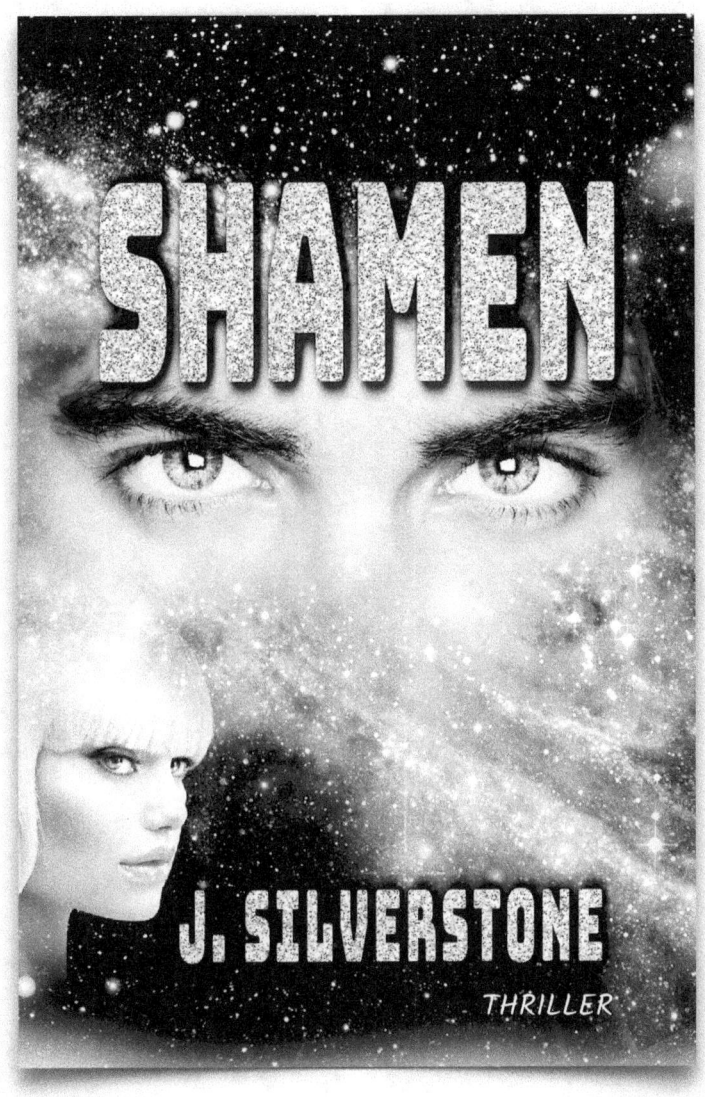

SHAMEN

J. SILVERSTONE

THRILLER

NEYTIRI PRESS

"THE UNIVERSE IS MENTAL"

HERMES TRISMEGISTUS
EGYPTIAN SCRIBE FOR THE GODS

~ THE KYBALION ~

TABLE OF CONTENTS

HISTORY

ASSIGNE: JENNY WEBSTER

PRIMARY INTEREST: SHAMEN

LOCATION: PLANET EARTH & BEYOND

CHRONICLER: J. SILVERSTONE

Sexual violence has long been used globally as a barbaric way to sow terror and assert control.

~ ASSOCIATED PRESS ~

CHAPTER ONE

On my back, feet facing up, I can't see anything other than the soft pink lining of what I later learn was my mother's womb.

As soon as the three-dimensional control of Planet Earth took me over, I forgot about the throbbing pink walls and the tingles and waves my fetal body was experiencing.

A cold rush went through me as my head touched what I later learned was cold. There was something else that came in and made a slight pressure at the sides of my head which I also later learned were hands in latex gloves.

A new environment, a new atmosphere was taking over the encasement growing around my body that had been in suspension for nine months. I only remember the journey out of that warm pink chamber into a new environment, changing a world of quiet growth for the rest of this new life.

I can't describe how or why I knew it was Shamen holding my head that brought me into this life, because I forgot about it till later. In fact, I didn't think about Shamen at all till he started following me at a time I was making my own decisions and feeling the empowerment of success.

Born with a good set of physical genes and guidance to places that make my quest possible, I had been buoyed by my good luck. However, when choices got difficult and negative events began to implant into my feelings, emotional scars surfaced and tested me once again.

When I travelled the globe for photo and film shoots, aspects of those past life experiences began to tickle my brain. At the beginning of my first European tour, before I was known in the States, I was walking top designer shows in Paris and Italy and getting a lot of notice. Shamen's music was the hit of the season and played at most of the shows. His music affected me like no other. It made me feel like I was an instrument, part of the band. For some reason he would change his tempo when I came on the runway which set my walk apart from the other models. Standing out I quickly became a Fashion Week star.

I knew there is a reason to connect with Shamen in such a personal way. It took me into a layer of impression I had forgotten that warned me to stop falling into the life path of another.

Early in this life a wise woman had warned me, "Never give up, no matter the temptation. Trust comes from the purity of the heart. Don't ignore but test your instincts. Beware emotion, keep objective. Be your own person."

Those words imbedded themselves into me. They've been guardrails for this journey in life.

Alone in New York with my mother, living a monastic kind of life, I avoided contact with nearly everybody when I wasn't working. I didn't go to parties, mother watched television day and night and when home from work, I studied for the classes I was taking at New York University.

At work I would ask for Shamen's music. Its familiarity motivated different states of mind. My career was in full swing. I never gave the musician Shamen a thought, but allowed the totality of his music to envelop me. It definitely influenced my super star rise in the fashion world.

Later, when I was planning my wedding, Shamen immediately came to mind. I arranged a meeting with the wedding planners, and we met on a holy mountain in New Mexico. There was a strong connection beyond the words we exchanged and later, when I went back in time, I learned we had a long and powerful history together. It had been a tsunami of emotions with feelings that never left me. I just couldn't identify the events that made them happen.

We had generations of history buried deep in our memories that the first breaths of new life wiped out. Sometimes however, fragments or larger pieces are left behind that aided or demanded attention.

The moment in life when we lose our experience and knowledge is probably the reason babies cry when they're born. Maybe they scream in protest or welcome the physical release. Some don't take their first breath, maybe wanting to keep their consciousness where it had been. It's usually forced, successfully.

In whatever way it comes, the first breath of air for Earth life is traumatic. Entry is a huge eraser, thrusting one into the experiences of new life and its tests till the truth of instinct is fully recognized. Some call that Karma, which means every action has a re-action. One pays or is paid for deeds that were positive or negative.

Coming back to Earth and the nanosecond consciousness when one realizes all information is gone, stays with most Earthlings. Something is missing. There must be more. No matter if dreams come true, there's a hole. But how can something not remembered make its non-presence felt? The answer is a hard place to reach, like an itch in the center of the back.

I don't remember much about my actual trip to Earth till the rebirthing time. Most of it was in a vacuum in which nothing interesting or amazing consciously happened. Unless I've forgotten it all because I was the subject of some natural or robotic force that put together parts, talents and understandings that create the physical body around the mental energy essentially and purely me;

DNA, the Double Helix that carries the blueprint of past and present from which we draw upon or repress.

Truth is, I don't remember much till I became aware of the glistening pink walls undulating around me. As I started to question their reality I hit that wall of cold air, continuing to slip away from the damp walls of the warm, comfortable place where my body had been growing.

Cold reality created a hard shell of purpose for living in this new world, moving me away from the comfortable familiarity I thought I would always have. That cold blast of air upon exiting my mother's womb left a strong impression on me. The shock of the enormous change of environment, a physical punch, forcing me to take a breath so I could exhale with an ear-piercing scream.

It took nearly a half lifetime to learn some of the awakenings to truths I've lost. Lessons learned and earned that surface when least expected. But for some reason, extraterrestrial or spiritual, they're rarely used, choosing instead to live once again through the experience. Learning the hard way – again.

When I slipped through the pink walls of my mother's birth canal, and the cold hit the top of my head, those slippery hands that supported my head as I came out were from centuries back. The bolt of knowledge hit me with a force I will never forget when I realized the hands touching me belonged to Shamen. His energy unlike any other I've encountered has never been questioned. It was always his, sometimes in ecstasy, many times in fear and pain.

In my last life I had been terrified when Shamen touched me. It was not in fear. I had been buried in an avalanche and he had come as an apparition to lead rescuers to dig and pull me out of the ice. I trusted him then. I had to. Or I would have been dead.

But I haven't remembered much of that till now. It's that bolt I feel every time I see him, the unexplainable excitement that catches my breath. The tingle and warmth that churns to dread when his darkness descends.

Time travel is new for me. I was beginning to have a feel for it in my last life but that was cut short. Too short and too violent and I'm not sure I want to remember it because I came off it with sorrow and fear. Probably I came back to the world too soon and didn't take the time to evaluate what I learned. Past experience is covered with a dark paintbrush that just allows little glimmers of what happened there. I'm not sure how long I'm going to be in this body and I hope it isn't taken from me like it had been in that terrible, frightening war.

Now, fresh from an earlier life, I'm curious to know what is going to happen in this new one. Sometimes I go back and forth to different lifetimes where some of the players are familiar. But I don't think I have ever lived this one before. Shamen is the transformational energy that ties it together even though the first cold, loud minutes on Planet Earth brought no inkling of familiarity, everything was new. With the exception of Shamen's essence that made me feel secure. Yet I'm anxious because he's here. There's a lesson to be learned.

I want to live a few years with the warm loving essence I had at the with the person chosen to be my mother. Her essence is my lifeline now. It is the comfort I needed after the war that knocked me down and broke my ties with joy. What had been home became a nightmare to teach me fear and anger and the use of both to survive.

I learned some incredible tricks in expanding awareness; of what the mind and the ethereal body can do even though the end of that life was hell. It was a black patch that cost a lot but also gave a lot of information that should have been easier to find. But of course, the ferocity cannot be explained in a way for others to understand. It must be felt, even if only in the imagination and emotions. Better than three-dimensional Earth reality.

Now I'm thrust into a reincarnation that will test me to see how much more ability I still need to survive. Survival is in our DNA and as energy it can't be destroyed. But it has to be accessed and strengthened. That was what my last life was about; learning to keep experience and knowledge in the dot of my essence, embracing the power to help me soar.

Maybe that's why while I'm eager to experience this new life, I'm concerned I may have to go back to my other lives. I would like to think I'm finished with what happened because I don't want to get stuck in past mistakes, fear and regret. That will hold me back. Negative energy can shut down survival if the need to survive isn't strong enough.

Lying on this cold hard table wrapped in a blanket so tight I can't move; I'm meeting my first test in this life. Thinking in fear. A trap.

Maybe I should not stay in this new life. I can hold my breath and go back to the past. As I cross my arms across my chest, I notice soft cream doeskin gloves covering my arms past my elbows. Feeling a little faint, I breathe deeply. I thought it was the tight blanket or the dread. But the gloves make me realize I'm wearing a dress with a bodice so tight I can barely breathe. No wonder I don't like tight clothing.

Catching my breath with this new revelation, my congratulatory insight makes my breath shorter and the whale bones lining the dress bodice tighten, making it difficult to breathe. Then I see the cause of the breathlessness and no longer attribute it to the whale bones. Bonding with my pounding heart and hot cheeks that must be bright red, I turn away as an elegant man approaches me. Unease nearly knocks me backward as I realize he is overpowering me with extraordinary good looks that are familiar, but I don't know why. He wears silk trousers and a platinum and silver embroidered waistcoat. He appears to be otherworldly that I lightly recognize from other lifetimes. Though I hear warnings buzzing like gnats around my head, I find the gorgeous man compelling.

Clarity of thought is being taken over by a wanting that erases past feelings and blurs conscious thinking. Once again, as in other lifetimes, I dismiss the unease and allow myself to be taken in by the exciting way he makes me feel. Tingles are running up and down my spine and once again, my body is out of control. Allowing it to do its thing I still manage to appear aloof. I refuse to get caught up in the physical part even though it quickly flashes in my consciousness how good it feels.

The man I think is Shamen intensifies his smile as he begins to take me over. Trying to stay objective my breathing is growing slow and deep. There's a strong damp pulse between my legs, which upsets my belief I had more control. If I can go out of body, I should be able to control this one when I'm in it. Obviously, my struggle isn't over. I still feel love and anger, fear and desire for this man who seems to accompany me in every lifetime I've had.

As he bends to take my hand a jolt confirms this man is Shamen. I can't pull away.

Giving me the illusion of strength, he gives me enough pull before he takes me back easily. It isn't the physical strength as much as his intoxication. I give in to him, as always...

We walk through the garden, his hand resting lightly on the small of my back which burns with his touch. He can feel that. I try to stay neutral, but I can't. That deep gentle trembling takes over my body. I strain toward him. It's so natural.

Believing he wants me he is gentle and careful, not forceful but strong. Lulling behavior that's given readily and passionately, I want to make him feel as wonderful as he makes me. We fit, tailored to complement the other. We make love again and again and again...

Jumping to the present I'm uncomfortably aware I've been living in the past. How much time since Shamen tried to kiss my hand? How many lifetimes, how many experiences and impressions and lasting life lessons have I gone through to get to this present and hopefully conscious way?

Grabbed by this first sensational touch of the present lifetime, I'm blasted with bile spilling into my stomach, struck in a blinding, split second realization that everything is different. I'll no longer have the knowledge it took decades and centuries to build. I'll have to re-assemble the ragged and torn pieces of past life information and rebuild it to gain the knowledge that resides in my soul.

Bright lights wink, setting mixed feelings of excitement and fear. Probably a throwback to the insensitivity of that cold hard light blinding my sight when I was born. No one thought I would be looking. They thought I couldn't see. Ha!

My eyes close involuntarily with the thought of that huge blast of reality, those first bright lights, my first big breath then my first big scream.

That helpless vulnerability with the realization no one understands me and nothing makes sense was my first entry to Planet Earth. Except for the nipple and its warm soft milk going through me, I had no other haven of comfort.

Questions don't stop while my body was sleeping. Is Shamen protection? He was important in the past. Our energy is familiar and intimate, yet something makes me fear the ties we have.

Shamen is an intimate stranger. I don't remember why or when we've been joined in extreme fear and pain. I searched for the power to do the things I now know how to do. In part, because of Shamen, I was forced to leave my body and learn I can come back.

Not being born with a "How To" manual of living on Planet Earth, I acknowledge the Earth is a world of three-dimensions where lives of different designs create the myriad energies of a multi-dimensional planet. These different dimensions also become difficult when dealing with lowered expectations.

As humans we use our sensations through contact with Earth's physical reality. My fear is I may have to go through the realities of some lurid experiences I've had. My *conscious* mind presses a button of fear and anger that releases a wail that doesn't stop. "Will I have to do that life all over again," I hear myself asking over and over again.

Life Lessons surge, teasing with vaporous promises of peace and calm. Joining with a younger self and sliding down a slippery slope, my consciousness joins with my genetic cocktail for this brand-new life.

Hope this isn't the wrong environment and as hard as the last life. Doubts stop the slide. Do I have a choice?

The emotional library stored in my unconscious reminds me I can choose to relive a life by bringing it to a believable surface. A little fear reminds me of the danger I may not be able to get out once I'm in. Given the choice I may have to try.

That might be the reason the hands that held me for the first time in this life were Shamen's. From the past and now, the present he's my entry to this new three-dimensional world after the cocoon of the womb.

Slippery yet strong and gentle, I trusted Shamen's hands What choice did I have? I'm helpless and he's in charge. My throat tightens and fear erupts into another wail and scream as a veil of tears covers my face. Remembering this was not the first time I felt those hands and energy, I knew how they made me feel in other lives.

Once again I'm compelled to understand and embrace the power and the meaning of Shamen in the past and now, the present where I may allow his magnetic pull to save him as he destroys me. Am I to sacrifice myself for the sake of my destroyer? Is there a Joan of Arc DNA of selflessness in one of my building blocks of life?

Confused and inconsolable I watch my life as I knew it, fade away. Shamen tests the blanket to make sure it's so tight my limbs can't move. It's not the warm cozy protection I just left and it doesn't hide the cold hard surface his hands have put me on. The metal comes up through the few layers of cloth meant to protect me from discomfort. It doesn't. Despair makes me cry. More softly now. What else can I do?

Getting no awareness, the bright lights of the room are shining and hurting my eyes. I keep them shut to protect them but their energy is going through my outer layers and making an impression on my eyes.

Somewhere in the depths of my programing I 'm reminded of a bad smelling scarf tied over my face. Eyes blocked from seeing. Hands and legs bound with wire so thin it cuts my skin if I push against them. With an attitude of servility, I appear to accept them and try to go out of body.

It may be the cold but I'm shaking with fear and exhaustion. No longer on a metal medical table I find myself locked in a standing cell, hearing screams and gunfire for what appears to be days and nights. I have no idea how long I've been in this box with the sounds of death my only connection to life.

I learned to leave my body and go to other places before this, but I'm so overcome with the three-dimensional drama of Earth I'm too grounded for the energy needed for astral travel. Also, I'm afraid if I leave, I won't be able to return at a conscious level. My voices whisper to stay calm.

Was I not calm enough when the Gestapo arrested me and locked me in this steel coffin with space only enough to stoop? How can I stay calm when it's total black and I see nothing and my legs are screaming with their strain. If not for the human screams, shouted orders and gunshots, this could be a sense deprivation tank where all sensory apparatus is gone. But that's a lifetime away. I already lived it and don't want to go back. I don't know where I want to go. Panic is overtaking me. I can't stop it.

Stay calm the Voices advise again. *Use extra sensory ability to ignore the fear that's interrupting the sense* of self.

A space creates when the body no longer guards the kernel of consciousness that can fly free. But Euphoria has a habit of tripping one up. I'm denied access to information and abilities from lifetimes that are stored in a space that could fit on the tip of a needle.

I had felt so confident walking across the square near the ghetto maybe days ago. I just had my short blond hair trimmed and it looked great. My chic silk dress clung to me as my long legs made its way. It's a high to look good and use that confidence as a cover to mask the fear thumping in the pit of my stomach. Trying to push away the dread someone might discover my head shots in this portfolio makes me urge myself forward, telling myself the information I bring for the ghetto with disappearing ink will work.

As if they read my thoughts, two sinewy men in long black leather coats cross the street and approach me. I smile to cover fear. Dressed for the part they telegraph evil. They are Gestapo.

"Do you have a job for me?" My flippant question is answered with a blow that knocks my attempt at confidence to the ground with me. Moving to either side the marionettes of malevolence efficiently grab each arm and pull me up. I shout with revulsion.

"You can't do this. Let go of me. You have no right."

The two men walk me to a waiting black sedan where I'm blindfolded. The journey isn't long to this cramped metal box where I'm pushed in.

After a short time I hear people crying, pleading, praying, shouting. Then the screams ending in mid-range with a metal blizzard of machine gun bullets. A strange moment of silence then a voice barks, "DIE TOTEN ENTFERNEN" remove the dead.

Trained to withstand torture, this reality is proving to be too much. I'm in a holding cell waiting to be shot. My head is splitting from this demonstration of a Universe that no longer sees light.

I hadn't known there were actually humans on the planet who reveled in such darkness. Who are unable to see the powerful energy of positive light. Confinement in this box opened a vision of two sides I never considered.

As if someone read my mind, the metal door opened and hands dragged me out. Squinting in the blazing day I see an overconfident man, his well fitted uniform molded over a hard, toned body. The perfect Aryan Nazi, he smiles with the assurance he can have what he wants.

"We read the information for your Jew friends. We've known what you were doing and have been following you to see who else is involved. Your Jew friends in the ghetto have already gone up in smoke."

Involuntarily I gasp and start to sink with sadness and rage, lowering my psyche to the noise and chaos of Planet Earth.

"We've saved you to tell us who's behind this criminal act" the Nazi poster of a man was saying. "After you tell me everything, I'll take you as a souvenir. Since you've been standing in your own shit you'll have to clean yourself. I can't have you near me."

"If I walk in shit its of your making," I spit back. He smiles, "Tell me who your boyfriend is or whoever sent you on these errands. I have some ideas for you after you give me the information."

"You're a pig." I try not to panic. He has pushed an emotional button. I try to get my breath to work.

If only I could get out of here by using the techniques I had been practicing for out of body travel. But my mind keeps going to the fear I'm going to get hurt and die. Even though my country is in ruins I want to live and bring it back to a normalcy where sanity prevails. Torn between reacting to these strange new sensations and wanting to stop the drain of knowledge and memory leaving my brain, I'm torn between going back to retrieve it or forward to learn more.

A blindfold is tightly put over my eyes and I'm walked maybe twenty feet from the box to the place where I imagine prisoners are forced to stand to be shot. My hands are wired behind my back and my legs tied above the knees. The wire is so tight it's like a tourniquet making my blood stop.

The click of guns. I look up and can barely see the branches of a tree above the smelly blindfold. It's the last thing I'm going to see in this life and one of the most beautiful I've ever noticed. I hear the bullets fire, feel a pounding in my chest.

I close my mind then feel hands touching me. Kicking and screaming I try to push them away, but I have no control till something soft and warm is urged into my mouth. A *nipple,* but at the moment I don't care what it's called as the warm sweet liquid fills my mouth and teaches me to swallow.

Warmth fills my body, memories of life as I've been knowing it peel away. Panic dissolves with the warm sweet milk into dull satisfaction, ending my need to keep memories and get more knowledge. I want to fill the hole in my psyche to satisfy lifetimes that lured me.

Supporting me as I slide into comfort, Shamen's essence comes back, igniting unnamable hope, erasing the pit in my awareness. And as I have before, I believe in his power and open to him remembering how his touch erases the pain.

CHAPTER TWO

I've been on Earth before. Snatched from what I had thought was my destiny, a reoccurring dream comes every night that feels so real I sometimes wake up in a cold sweat, fearing it could come back.

Certain past life events are hard to see, but I remember standing against a wall, hands tied with wire behind my back. A slight bulge in the smelly blindfold covering my eyes lets me see a beautiful tree, its long thin branches bending to cover the horror beneath it. That tree is still in my mind. So is the powerful explosion that smacked something hot and hard into the center of my forehead and chest. The blow blossoming into a profusion of red as I fall through the colors of experience, levels of lives as I grasp for the white light before everything goes black.

I'm not sure how much I have lived between the past time of recollections and the present. Fearful of going back to fill missing chunks, I could make the same or new mistakes that would trap me on Earth again.

The one thing I'm sure I learned from those faults it's not easy to maintain objectivity over emotion when the body takes control. To keep discipline and focus when being whipped, betrayed, or murdered, requires a powerful inner core that will not allow external forces to rule. It's all about doing the work and not giving in to negative forces that want control.

It's that unsatisfied itch in the center of the back that requires focus and the ability to hear beyond Earth reality. So I listen when the Voices tell me to watch Shamen direct energy to incite good and evil.

I've been through hell and ecstasy with Shamen and I know he's difficult to escape. The remembrance of the ecstasy then the hell he put me through was nearly unbearable. The voices got me through, saved me lifetimes of reincarnations or body changes to reach the point I'm at now.

To say Shamen gets under my skin is a fair description of the way I feel when I'm close to him. Drawing me in like a magnet my body gets super sensitive, focusing beyond the reactive forces of Earth where it's easy to lose everything.

Leaving fetal growth and becoming a viable human, energizes the deep conscious knowledge that distributes secrets into our DNA. The force of the energy creates seekers searching for the ultimate answer to a question they don't know what to ask. *Is this it? Nothing more?*

Trying to find the answers to these questions may not be the kind of life I should have chosen for myself. But I was in such a hurry to get back to Earth and fight the evil that eliminated me for my beliefs, I took the first brain ride without having a plan, without thinking.

This birthing experience is different from the ones I've had before. I remember knowing all this in those first few hours, or maybe it was minutes before it all went away. Knowledge of knowing the loss I couldn't name kept me crying, even as the person called *mother* tried to comfort me.

Eight or ten years later I tried to explain to mother that babies cry when they're born because they're scared of what they see and they're probably cold.

"Babies can't see when they're born," Mother patted my hand with sweet indulgence.

"I did. But the bright lights hurt so I shut them tight." I explained. "Hands forced them open and dropped burning liquid into them. I screamed from the pain, but no one cared. They ignored me, touching me like I didn't feel what they were doing. No one listened to my cry for help."

"I'm sure you were comforted." Mother smiled and patted my hand again. I didn't tell her that not till Shamen lifted me from the table and held me close did I feel secure. But Mother was backing away.

"Darling, you have an over-active imagination," she tossed as she left the room.

"Shall I tell you what the Delivery room looked like?" I called to her retreating back.

She shook her head firmly. Palms up, little giggle, "It's enough!" Her reactions confirmed discomfort with my words. But maybe I'm believing my own fantasies. How can it be proven the things I say are real? Does the thought or re-creation of an event make it real? Creations in words, shapes or musical notations come from imagination. When those creative ideas come out in the open, they become their own identity, a sensation that provides a chain to feelings. Thoughts once spoken or written, painting and sculpture once ideas, become three-dimensional reality. When they land with density, it determines their power.

Wind is an obvious changing of energy form. If each particle of DNA retains individual consciousness, it ultimately merges into the singularity of the Universe where it all becomes whole.

But I'm getting way ahead of myself. I'm being born and aware of what the birth process is making me lose, and at the same time I'm seeing this happen totally outside of myself. Being born under the sign of Gemini – the planet of duality, I go through a schizophrenic bombardment as I watch my knowledge pushed away by new information gushing in. releasing words that create their own destiny.

Since our last meeting Shamen stays in my thoughts, circling around the parameter of my head and sliding into my brain at an opening of consciousness. He may have been the reason I left that small undulating cave of my mother's womb and slid into his hands. I knew in some outer space-conscious way that he was waiting for me. I expected him. He was my guide. The moment I felt his touch I knew it was Shamen. It was immediate. I knew it was him.

Did I know this was going to happen? Did I believe he was standing, waiting for me to slide out of my mother's womb? Maybe. I don't remember exactly because nothing is familiar in this new world of life except Shamen.

Feeling him more than recognizing him is the spark that opened my mind to activate something that empowers me to learn. Another emotional roller coaster ride to shake my sensibilities into a more powerful way for this livestream episode of my dream come true.

Going toward the nameless because words can't encapsulate what's in store, I put everything on faith. What choice is there anyway beside a destination to which we have no control. No one's life departure has a destination ticket written on it.

It would be so much faster and easier if we could find those answers immediately. Go straight to consciousness. But it seems impossible without the actual emotional experience of lessons that cement the path to goals. As of now I think I understand the kind of all encompassing energy to go out of body and come back in again.

The big conundrum, the nagging problem, is this love/hate thing I've had with Shamen for centuries. This time Shamen delivered me. He could have done something to end my life or made it difficult by crippling or disfiguring me. He didn't. Yet I still don't trust him.

He projects light yet he has darkness, a portrait of good and evil. I'd like to believe there is a compelling dark force over which he has no control and is essentially a good person. But that kind of thinking is only valid if Shamen is human and not a hologram or robot or even worse, a figment of my imagination. To deal with him is to balance on a bridge over a booby-trapped highway of morals.

After my birth I watched as he peeled off his slippery gloves and threw them into something and walked away. I cried again. I don't trust him, but I didn't want him to leave.

My cries to cover his loss demanded something take its place. Nice warm milk was good, but I wanted the warmth of another skin, another energy to touch me and fill the hole in my soul. I understood at that moment of vulnerability that love is energy for strength and support.

I had that feeling from the time I was born. Once, unable to move because I was so newly born, I lay in a crib, unable to raise my head. The young human with the title, Sister, was leaning over the bars of the crib staring down as she kneaded a pillow in her hands. Only four years old, her face flushed, eyes unblinking made me recognize a malice that scared me.

She was going to put that pink pillow over my face so I couldn't breathe. Zipped into a new age jumpsuit that kept me from freedom, my short time on Earth was about to end as that four-year-old sister thought about clearing her territory. Before she could act, having nothing but my voice, I shrieked.

The piercing scream brought my mother into the room in time to see my sister drop the pillow. With a calming caress to my forehead she escorted my sister out of the room toward the kitchen for milk and cookies.

As I thought my mother was coming back into the room I heard a scream, but rotors of a helicopter drowned out that sound and I found myself strapped into the seat of a huge, noisy helicopter tilting toward a group of hippies and I wonder if I'm time traveling back to the Sixties. But then I see the tall blonde man standing in the opening, waiting. Our eyes meet. His energy hits me in the heart and in a clear flash a force carried by the wind of the helicopter blades I'm sent to a new reality that unites with Shamen.

Recognition continues to vibrate as I see Shamen's tanned fit body poured into tight jeans like a second skin. His physique has the power, shape and weight of a dancer and his light blue cotton shirt threaded with gold is backlit by the sun, making him glow. An incredible photo opportunity, he becomes a snapshot in my mind.

Putting his hand out to shake mine I want to pull away. I don't want his flesh touching mine. It will make him too real. What is this emotional tango I struggle with? That instant hit of his physical beauty and that strong yet pliable body awakening a longing to have him fold me into his arms and be comforted by him, makes me happy.

A message intervenes with my emotions and warns me; *stay away. He'll melt you.* A lifetime that makes itself real was when I was on the cusp of breaking through to global fame as a super model, walking a fashion show for a dear friend and one of the hottest designers of the season, June Tauber. She loved the way I looked in her designs and in a delirious short time I was to make my first Vogue cover in a June Tauber gown. This fashion show was to be June's first world-wide streaming.

Wearing ridiculously high shoes based on the design of a Chiopine, a two-foot wood shoe that looks like a tree stump with straps worn by noble Venetian women in the late 1500s. More like a vision from Mars was the two iridescently lighted bands of green Lycra fashioned into a bikini. The ensemble is covered with a transparent silk veil cascading from the top of an emerald crown on my head to the tips of the Chiopine shoes. I had practiced walking in those shoes with the veil for a few hours as I was afraid the veil might get caught or I'd lose my balance and sprawl on to the runway.

In any event the fashion press embraced June's P.R. release and looked forward to seeing the ultimate, ground-breaking wedding gown of the season. The new IT look.

I thought it was a joke, but June had been good to me when I first got into modeling and I couldn't disappoint her. Still, I was breathing hard and trying to keep my nerves in control as I waited for my grand entrance – the last outfit of a show that sounded like it had been a huge success so far.

Over the murmur of voices and laughter, a piercing electronic harp and guitar made the fashion elite drop their gossip and focus on the music erupting in the darkness.

A four-foot slash of white light became the gateway for me to emerge from the dark. Lights pinpoint my emerald crown and I take a few deep breaths to still my quivering nerves.

A lot is riding on this walk down the runway in perilous shoes few humans in this Century could wear. The wedding gown is one of the most coveted attention getters in the modeling world. My task was to make it to the front of the runway and back, appearing to look as carefree and glamorous without falling.

Focusing on Shamen's music to keep me in the groove I let it take me over with an intensity that directed my nerves to feel exhilaration rather than fear.

Light blanketed me, gratefully separating me from the audience on either side as I make my way on the runway of light in impossibly high shoes and a nearly nude costume.

The music as my source of strength engaged me to twist and stretch, the flimsy veil a prop for my hands and faith in my balance. Warily keeping my balance in the center of the white light, I became a feline stalking my prey. The music followed becoming a set of moments where movement and sound become one.

Not even a breath or soft cough was heard as the rapt audience held their breath for the wobble, the fall, something to happen with those stilts and wisps of fabric floating above them. But using muscle discipline and sheer will to keep the sparkling bandeaus in place, I became an instant media thrill, "*a sinuous cat achieves the impossible*" were headlines across the world. Only the language changed as my face and body became the international trademark for JUNE.

Consequently, I was able to deposit a large check as an advance on media royalties for that single jaunt in June's wedding gown, turning me into a super model and Shamen a rock star. A mutual rise to fame from eons to connect again.

If we know the future, maybe we can change mistakes before they happen. Though considering the circumstances under which I made countless mistakes over the centuries, I can't think of one I would have changed. They were gifts, an opportunity to learn. Wake-up calls.

In that past life I was earning a lot of money and surrounded by smart, tough people for protection and career.

Yet with all those guards and good luck, I slid down a trap opened by hubris. A choice made without thought turned my life upside down. I don't remember the individual events, only that so much had been handed to me; photogenic looks, lean graceful body and the ability to morph from innocence to bombshell – always leaving a piece of the opposite behind.

When I think of the good people around me that made my successful career happen, it's burdened with loss and guilt. What did I do? Am I paying for past behavior?

I thought I knew and understood the dangers in the fashion world and jeopardy would not touch me. I was *anointed*. Nothing could affect me. Surviving a difficult childhood I believed I had paid my dues. Life should be good once I was on my way. Belief began to crumble after several famous commercials when my agency suggested I take acting lessons as there had been lots of calls about me for film roles.

Based on reputation and his flirt with fame I had recognized Lawrence Standon's name before I met him in his present incarnation as an acting coach. Because he felt familiar, I argued with myself that I'm making up my inner voice when it told me to be careful with Standon. Believing he held the key to what I needed for an acting career I was flattered and excited he singled me out when I used my beautiful mask to impress him and get his acceptance. I found success as a model and now I would do it as an actress.

My brain drew a curtain over reason and allowed gullible innocence to take over. When Standon told me I had to manage my imagination to make my presence felt in film, I wasn't sure what he was talking about, but I liked his attention and believed he would lead me to the answer.

Young and beautiful, having doors opened because of my looks, I had no clue Standon, would want to do anything other than help me as everyone had since I was discovered not that long ago. Flushed with success and feeling as if I could do anything Standon would be the key to a step up the ladder of success as an actor and I was thrilled when he offered to coach me privately.

Meeting at his studio I was surprised when we got in his car and drove to a run down, tawdry motel, "*for atmosphere*" he explained.

"It looks like a B movie set," I said, hoping he would say it was.

"You need to get down and dirty and away from that innocent purity you sell. You need to live in the moment without prejudgments."

Clueless, feeling insecure and wanting *to be in the moment*, I took the sexy black bathing suit Standon handed me, explaining I needed more provocative pictures for my portfolio.

Up till then I was getting lots of great shots from famous photographers where we pushed the walls of commercialism for experimentation and fun. The shots were incredible and I wondered if there was a difference between a model and an actor's photographs.

Nevertheless, I told Standon I thought the bathing suit made up of thin straps that barely covered any of my private parts was not flattering and I didn't want to be photographed in it.

"If you want to be an actress you've got to make it one of the sexiest most desirable bathing suits of all time. You know how to do it visually, now I want you to do it emotionally. Make me feel it. Turn my feelings on with your own.

Recoiling and without hesitation I protested.

"I'm not going to wear this. It's tawdry and exploitative. This is not what makes a woman sexy."

"You are the sexiest woman in the world. You've worn sexier than this."

He was right but the circumstances were different. I'm here alone with this person I don't know other than what I think of him. Blocking the voices screaming at me to *listen and don't put the bathing suit on.*

Determined to do what I have to in order to be an actress, I went into the small, not very clean bathroom and put the bathing suit on, careful to cover as much of myself as I could. Tying my cashmere hoodie around my waist I open the door to Standon waiting with two crystal glasses filled with champagne. Handing me one, he smiled. A look I didn't totally believe.

"Have us feel what you're experiencing so we'll believe it. Here. Drink it, use it to sell us your excitement."

"I don't drink alcohol. Sparkling water will work".

"I don't have anything else to put in the glass." Annoyance coated his words. "We need the bubbles. Fake it. You want to be an actress. Take a sip and enjoy it. Tease the camera with the champagne. Make us feel that bathing suit is enhancing one of the most incredible bodies on the planet. Take a sip. It will connect you to your feelings. Flirt with it, make it want you by teasing how much more you have to give. Give yourself to the camera."

I hear his words as clearly now as I did that Saturday afternoon when I was making every mistake in the book. Innocent and ignoring another message in my head telling me to get out. I didn't listen and stayed as the champaign went straight to my head.

At first, I was unsure if anything was wrong. I could still think. But I had to pose with ridiculous five-inch stiletto heels with ties to my knees below a bathing suit with little more coverage then the straps. I was torn between my desire to perform, and my moral training telling me this wasn't right. *This is not about acting,* came the message in my head. *It's Standon's amateur photo shoot.*

"Lean into this. You're gorgeous when you're angry. You're a panther." He jumped on the bed and smiling behind the black Hasselblad he photographed me fighting to get away. It was funny for him.

Amusing for him. A lesson for me. Recalling the incident I remember feeling my empowerment disappear. Standon was dismissive. "Lean in toward the camera," he was saying. "Lick your lips, feel your body under that bathing suit, how it wants to come out."

My head spins. My breath, stops.

"Take another sip while you look at the camera," he orders. "You're beautiful. Feel that power in your breasts, between your legs where it's tingling and wet."

He was stroking himself. I couldn't believe what he was doing. Feeling panic, I started to get up but his strong hands sprang for my shoulders and pushed me down.

"Don't move," commanded his announcer type voice. I twisted away. His arm shot out and held me back.

"You were enthusiastic when I asked if you'd like coaching."

There was so much I wanted to say but held back. I wanted to get out, but nothing had happened except to put on a revealing bathing suit. This was fake and I fell for it. I had to get away.

"I don't feel well. I'd like to go home," popped out of my mouth. "I'd be mortified if I was sick in front of you," I lied.

Dropping my arm and backing away, he wanted to get away from me. My best acting yet! In his way he was a good acting teacher though I would no longer go to his class. Actually I'd had enough of the acting world. Modeling was safer.

As I gratefully got home my phone rang and the bottom fell out of this reality and entered a sharpened awareness as the voice of Shamen came through the lines. With relief his melodious hypnotizing words gave me a ticket to board his emotional roller coaster. Grateful to change the scenery I stepped right on, hoping this ride would be a good one.

Remember the other times kicked into my head. I didn't want to remember them, but I did feel a sinking in my gut and found myself back on the edge of a cliff, consumed by loneliness, facing an abyss of good or bad from which to choose. To stay on Earth's wheel of survival and its rule of Karma, the kaleidoscope of choice, or let go and fly into the Universe and forget the task I returned to do.

I was walking into what Don Juan in *the book* bearing his name called, *controlled folly*, doing something you know won't work, but you do it anyway.

Though I'm not paying much attention to the feelings that come up from my time past I do know that once again, in this lifetime I'm drawn in by Shamen's mystique and understanding of himself and how he affects others. He has an energy so intense I feel at times I can merge with him.

However, having experienced the tunnels that can be taken on planet Earth I keep a cautious and respectful distance of Shamen's abilities. Light or dark, he has the power to move me toward a new level of myself. Most times I had to learn in the worst way, but the lessons brought me a semblance of understanding and light.

It's frightening to know in that split second of enlightenment as I'm being placed on a cold hard table after leaving the warmth of my mother's womb, I will have to make myself knowledgeable again and re-live so many of the tests of past life lessons. I thought I had moved on from those trials. Yet it appears the road toward that elusive place I seek, is still too far for me to avoid the pitfalls that make me stop my journey toward what I think I know, but is actually unknown.

Shamen knows my goals and has exposed and dangled the potential of a lighted way many times. Too often I fell for it. Even now, though I know better, there is still a little place in my head that sends out the message he can guide me toward a successful goal. Once again, my "controlled folly".

And because I can't remember much of the dark holes I embraced and the emotional experiences that helped me grow I stand backstage, trying to control anxiety and slow my breath as I prepare to go out on the runway for my first big New York fashion show.

Less than a month after moving to the city, getting comfortable with its beat and energy, I get a prime assignment, the opening of fashion week and I'm yo walk one of the most important designer shows of the year. Everything seemed perfect – I was living the kind of life I had read about in fashion magazines, and now I was one of "them" – living and looking like a model in pictures on screens around the world.

Hefting my portfolio and oversized Balenciaga bag stuffed with hair pieces, shoes and accessories, I made rounds to introduce myself to the editorial and commercial world of fashion photography.

"Making rounds" is an intense whirlwind on busy New York streets too jammed to drive. Circling slower pedestrians, I have to run to appointments with as little damage to my makeup and hair as possible. Lacking experience, I'm caught in the mindless whirlwind of demands for attitude on command while looking gorgeous and staying in control within the midst of a bewildering bombardment of sensations.

Learning the ropes of a fashion model I had spent weeks working as a runway model at the international fashion shows in Europe. Much of its coverage hit the U.S. market so my face was getting known before I worked there.

The work of fashion is an exhausting trek. Often after being on location at sunrise, the end of a day I'd fall into a dreamless sleep and wake up not recognizing the room, country or time I was in. Using tricks I learned a lifetime ago, I did deep breathing till I remembered what I was supposed to do and where I was supposed to go.

And now this first big exposure in the United States will get millions of viewers. It's make-or-break time.

Since arriving in New York, I got lots of attention thanks to my cookie cutter looks and a camera attitude that gravitates from *innocence to* sexy. Most importantly, I had a great agent who knew exactly how to market me. I owe everything to her and to Verruno, the famous fashion photographer who discovered me behind the counter of a clothing store and asked to take my picture.

Tragically, though I owed my agent everything, her reward was to be murdered in the back seat of a taxicab by people who thought they owned me.

Her murder is one of the memories that didn't get erased in this new life. It's a burden that brings strong feelings of guilt and regret which I don't totally understand. In three-dimensional reality, it was my actions that got her killed. I'm pretty sure that's true, otherwise why would I feel guilty? I should have resigned from the agency, walked away, saved her life.

But my confidence in her strength and power got her killed. A lifetime ago that horrible moment in time taught me some powerful and hard lessons. Even though, no matter how much I believe in destiny and no matter which side of the happy or sad scale I'm on, I'll never forgive myself for her death. I carry it with me as a black mark on my quest.

I met Shamen before I remembered the wrong turns of my past. This time, meeting at the start of our careers with everything so new and exciting I paid no attention to the signs I should have recognized from the past. But Shamen's primal yet familiar music was so compelling, I responded to it with a hunger that connected me to its creator.

At first, I didn't recognize the warning signals tapping at my brain. Bolts of uncomfortable energy permeating the unconscious to be alert. I ignored them by tamping them out with the pleasure gene. Intellectual knowledge doesn't control feelings. It can affect emotion, but whatever the trigger, feelings usually take center stage. The answer is to be aware of alien feelings. Don't let them take over before you can't stop them. The head must work in tandem with the heart.

I didn't recognize my romanticized reaction to a contemporary god figure till emotions tore me up. It took a new lifetime to test out the mastery of my emotions. Learning when I have them in control, I get closer to the point where truth is the ultimate standard. There is only one truth, no matter how many fractures emanate from it.

Still, after all these lifetimes Shamen is difficult to understand. This beautifully formed assemblage of thoughts, feelings and magnetic energy have made me wonder all this time if he is human or powered by Artificial Intelligence – A.I. a robot, or a hologram of desire.

His influence over that *feel good belief* generated a treasure trove for him and his handlers. Whether genetic or manufactured, Shamen's personality and talent was a trajectory to rock stardom that took milliseconds. A compelling young Adonis released to mass consciousness with an energy that surges angelic innocence and oozing sex, he is instant satisfaction for those who experience him.

Of course, this is my initial report. Who knows what the future may bring to my agenda of understanding Shamen's significance in life and whether he is a human or an incredible Artificial Intelligence specimen.

Bottom line, Shamen can easily be a non-mortal. The more I watch him the more I accept my first instinct that he's a robot or maybe an angel. If sent from an interplanetary space he has been able to create a following so powerful he can magnetize and draw the world into a single mind thought.

There have been those with the magnetic power to draw masses into the dark. Hitler lured the German masses to believe as fervently in his dark declarations as their opposites believed in the light. Till this time, those that herald the dark, last only a comparatively short time. Most have ended badly.

Shamen may have more power than the despots on Planet Earth and has come to capture the planet for some reason we have yet to learn.

Science has created DNA programs attached to human brains that counter a magnetism such as Shamen's. So far, they haven't been totally successful because genetic human breeding imbeds a need for idolatry. Shamen is filling that role as a throwback hippie from the Sangre de Christo mountains of New Mexico.

Humans, the main force on Planet Earth have been in battle with Gaia, Planet Earth's mother, who every once in awhile proves that the one who controls the elements controls Planet Earth. Gaia can dial in any excess like temperature control to destroy all life on the planet that would take millions of years to regenerate from ice or overheating.

If only Shamen could be programmed with a good/bad switch to enhance his mortal or robotic awareness of enlightenment or evil, evolution or destruction. Whatever his program, my mission is to discover its purpose. My hope is the physical or technical can be controlled for the good.

Looking out the window of the helicopter before its final descent toward one of the most spiritual places on Earth, I see ramshackle huts and begin to travel out of body to a flat dark field where I see through the window of one of the shacks. If I had my body, the hair on the back of my neck would be standing up at the chilling sight of a circle of older men and a nude terrified girl in the center, shaking as she tries to cover herself.

Sweeping in as close as possible I smell the dank mustiness of wool mingling with the damp odor of masculine sweat that surrounds her. There is no escaping the rumbling cadence of their voices, a nest of Hornets, underscoring the terror and loneliness of the young innocent whose crime was being born with the consciousness she carries.

My heart dictating my path I zoom in to see the young woman is my sister Amanda from many lifetimes past. We have been mirrors for each other and have exchanged positions. This is not Amanda's first torture. Once again, she doesn't understand why it's happening. I feel her fear. Held by a coven of men, she is crying, straining to get away, but they won't let her go.

I try sending her a message to transcend the reality. 16th Century Jewish folklore says because of past sins a disembodied human spirit called a Dybbuk wanders until it finds a haven in the body of a living, pure person. It's what the coven says they will remove from Amanda.

I pray in this incarnation Amanda will not freeze and become catatonic as she has in the past. She keeps repeating this lesson and fails to understand it's her opportunity to rise above physical restraints and elevate to a higher place, a more inspired understanding that would allow her the next level of consciousness. But terror makes her stay in the darkness she is dissolving into now. She's had the training and I know she hears the inner voices. But fear directs her and she refuses to accept the voices as her own.

I will myself away from the young woman as the men gather closer to clear what they say is her demonic presence. She won't survive but hopefully this will lead her to a new, positive level.

Turning back, I see them putting her in a plain wooden box, arms crossed over her breast, her eyes closed in the classic pose of the dead. But she's alive, breathing. I hope she recognizes the voices in her head coming from interstellar teachers to train her for higher levels so she won't suffer.

One of the men in the circle lifts his head and turns to look at me, breaking through the layers of energy that should be hiding my essence. He is the only one who knows I'm here. I stop what feels like breathing. Within this frightening tableau of indecency is a smoldering, smirking, Shamen, radiating as human. Appearing so innocent and sexy I wonder if it's possible to program a robot to have the kind of energy he emanates. Maybe he's a demon from the lowest depths of the planet where the energy of gravity keeps humans planted on Earth instead of free to roam the Universe.

Shamen's disarming energy is alluring and sexy. Like ice cream, he satisfies a craving you don't know you have till you taste it.

Making a strong first impression that grew overnight with release of his first album and the live stream global concert, his popularity was cataclysmic, affecting everyone in some way.

Holographic memories of our past lives together are popping up and sparking my memory of methods I used to survive. "Out of body" known as *OOB* was the first big one. At first I thought going out of my body meant I was dead. Then I learned to focus, sometimes in primitive ways, and my ability grew more polished and immediate as years progressed.

To start I'd visit people, learn about them, and give help if needed. That kind of help however is cautioned by the Voices advising it creates expectation that can result in deep disappointment. This causes a negative stoppage on one's journey through life. The guides tell me to stay the observer and allow others to live their own truth. But it's hard not to help even though both sides are ingrained in me.

My sister, Amanda, is a good example. She has been blocked by her own mind, fighting for what she believes is truth. But she refuses to stop and take a breath and ask what it means.

We're separate though I feel her helplessness as she lays stripped and cold in a pine box *to rid her of demons.* Those *demons,* her beliefs, will not be excised from her. Consequently she pays physically and emotionally as she tries to warn the world of darkness threatening planet Earth.

Wishing I could accelerate her to rise above the physical, I still feel the glow of pride for her courage and conviction.

With disdain written on his face, I watch Shamen melt and transform into a younger version of himself wearing the long white coat of a doctor. Struggling with the frenzied twists and turns of Amanda, now wearing a thin grey tunic with thick leather snake guards covering her ankles to her knees, she tries with every bit of energy she has to twist away from the hypodermic he holds in his hand.

Chained and unable to move far enough away, Shamen injects her with a small amount of some drug he is using to wipe away centuries of belief Amanda carries in her soul. They might succeed in re-wiring her to be as adamant as she was in her beliefs to embrace the opposite conviction that Planet Earth is not in danger of plunging into darkness to another ice age. Though I doubt it.

The method these men are implementing is a way to keep the public quiet and content in their belief they will always be safe. Unaware their neighbors and even people in their own families, are essentially *bio-conformed humans* who are wired for their thoughts, words and actions. They don't have the ability to access most concepts as they are programmed to dismiss original thought. Dictators have tried for centuries on Planet Earth to make their public behave in this way, but its only with the advent of the Bioconformed biology that uses human parts and the latest electronic impulses that this was achieved.

Before her abduction Amanda was writing editorials warning of the danger in following the dictates of a single person, especially those who say they hold secrets no others have.

"There will be many whose words and actions light the way to truth," she wrote. *"This will dispel darkness and keep our hearts working in tangent with our brain to keep the path solid and straight,"* she tried to explain.

Believing the demands of the heart and mind will convey the message, Amanda preached to those who wanted to hear her comforting explanation that there is more than one guide in a lifetime.

Proud of Amanda's bravery and sacrifice, her pain is a hole in my soul. Conditioned to help others by staying out of sight and sending energy so they can learn for themselves I was warned if I step in, Amanda would be dependent for centuries. She has to find power herself.

Having traded lives I understand she's now on an emotional slide into a black hole that won't stop till she finds her brakes to stop it. I can't follow her because she won't listen, ignoring the lifetimes I tried to plant suggestion in her.

I lost track of Amanda the last time around in the journey of my past life. I embraced energy, the exciting kind. I lived life pretending to have a great time in attitudes that spilled from seamless paper to two-dimensional reality that was familiar to me because of my fantasy work.

My working "family" as I grew to perceive fellow models, were gorgeous and able to look genuinely happy. Till the looks got stiff and the fun became boring. Then came the insidious emptiness and unnamable hunger that gnawed for clarity, dove tailing into pain and terror to an epiphany that brought me to cleanse my soul. It was from that low point I learned to keep my conscious awareness that let me go out of body. What a gift of freedom, knowing from the onset it could not be abused. Lessons from negative energy are long and strong when coming through the pathway of trauma.

I had been a totem for the seduction and destruction of innocents. And within that desperate situation I was given the gift of light, the gateway in the midst of pain to see a path away from physical destruction to freedom.

Through the centuries I learned the lessons were at times the biggest enemy, yet the best teacher. The more powerful the incident, the deeper the resonance. My default was to find the way forward with light, a beacon I visualized to be in the center of my forehead.

I only wish I had been able to energize Amanda with that light and cut through the layers to infuse her with what I know.

Shamen came close, destroying my connection to the young girl closed in a wooden box. Breathing rapidly, quivering with cold and fear, I pull away from the pain. Unsettling to watch a carbon copy of myself making what is essentially self-inflicted mistakes. Sending the most golden rays of positive energy, to Amanda, I draw away, grateful I don't have to live through that again.

Yet an energy inside me doesn't want to leave the womb of Earth. It has secrets I want to learn. Knowledge learned among the bumpy crevices and hills of Earth's emotional landscape are the fast track to get to what some call *the promised land.*

But like all the other lives I can remember, just as I'm getting my life together and finally recognizing what my goal is at the time, a force knocks me off the path. This time it was an adulation and freedom I'd never known before.

Not long-ago Shamen and I had been the living manifestation of perfection. For a time, I believed it. But now, on the journey to my promised land, Shamen comes from centuries of challenge to destroy or test my skills again.

In past lives we had different names, and many times I was madly in love with him. When we met this time, there was a familiarity, a reunion with an old friend, or enemy. He came back into my life after deceit and unimaginable lies had roped me into a fantasy that became a nightmare.

And now he is a blond-haired Adonis jousting with some of the darkest elements on Planet Earth to control the messaging of the planet. I fear this message will take us to destruction.

The man's appearance is so perfect he could easily be a neo-humanoid – a being who exists through thought, a reality only in the mind, a physical that is actually a dream.

In the future maybe not too far away, if Earth becomes too dangerous for its sentient beings, we will all become thought forms with no physical reality other than the one we reflect to others. We'll be gaseous vapors of thought with extending physical reactions to enhance the experience. Vapor or hard-edged reality, falling off the path is never a big deal. It's an experience to heighten perception.

I've been training to use techniques and instincts to connect with my primal source. It has taken years of lifetimes and inner voices guiding me to connect with the power to be free. Sometimes the power is shattered by another lesson from the Universe to clear cobwebs before entering the higher levels of consciousness.

And Shamen has the power to shatter that magic. His music crisscrossed every place I worked, no matter the circumstance. He would come on a screen or walk on to a stage and everything would stop as if he held the power for others to breathe. Designers loved his music and I was in nearly every big fashion show that used his music for the runway. Rarely speaking to each other in public and never physically connecting after the shows, we were still a team. Dressed in fabulous clothes, moving to his music that was controlling my walk I felt as if we were making love, connecting with a frenzy though physically apart.

I was eighteen years old, a virgin, allowing myself to expose feelings in the spotlight because it felt good. People liked my characters and paid me a lot of money to have fun playing with them. Shamen was all about control, connecting through music and emotion. Expectations of touch moved through Shamen's music to make me float along the geometric of the runway, my body an instrument to enhance the sounds as they affected me in the most sensuous ways.

His music invaded me, controlled my emotions and energy. It made my walk distinct from the other models, a distinction quickly elevating me to fame that was more lucrative than I ever dreamed. Yet the best gift was creative acceptance. Agreement that what feels good for me, works for others. Almost everything I put out was accepted as reality, even my fantasies. My personal world and its manifestations became real. Celebrities wanted friendship and to my surprise were deferential. With constant recognition and attention, the exciting weeks and months flew by till I forgot the mission I had come to Earth to accomplish.

I was living Earth life rather than filling it with what I had been sent – to learn the reason Shamen is here, what he plans, how much power he has and who controls it? Does he have an on-off switch if his humanity gets too brutal? Is he a superhuman with the ability to turn the planet away from doom, or a malignant force guiding it to destruction?

As a supermodel, life was filled with one high to another. I had achieved my ideal to look like the Swans and Cranes I'd seen flying in the Stratosphere that initially I thought were fantasy. In Tibet I learned the birds were actually flying into the outer layers of energy circling Earth as I joined them.

Meanwhile on solid Earth, Shamen's fame was on fast forward along with my own. His music inspired me yet there was something making me want to keep him away. He scared me, but I did not want that to get in my way. Everything in life is preordained and our only choice is perception. I didn't think we could be controlled by outer forces till later when I experienced it myself.

Young and heady with the excitement of being a superstar, for the first time I had money to spend and I wasn't thinking about outer forces, self-discipline, or control.

Not having to go through the ranks of exposure for work, I became well known from the first photo shoots and designer fashion shows I walked. The careful marketing procedures, the foundation of the vast international exposure, were being done by a pair of brilliant salesmen I never knew existed till nearly ten years of being controlled by them. Bernstein and Kalman the best publicists in the world were made known to me when they gave me a job that had been set up to meet the man I was to marry. They, along with a small group of power brokers, had chosen this man to control the world.

I learned the truth after that lifetime which impressed upon me the importance of honing my skills to see into the future instead of re-living the past.

Not yet conscious of the power of my spiritual energy I had been living with Earth's three-dimensional awareness and controlled by the gravitational power of planet Earth. Pressured to look and feel the way clients in the advertising and editorial world hired me to be, I essentially became a well-paid putty machine for someone's vision, unaware of the me inside the brain that was hidden by my face.

Admittedly I love to dress up and especially make lots of money doing it. I no longer had to worry about finances or having to make decisions based on need. I had earned enough to live off investments and no longer experience the fear of not knowing if I would have enough to take care of my mother, an uncomfortable and scary position when facing a darkening void.

Having worried for a long time about my mother's welfare, my greatest joy is knowing I had set her up in a safe and comfortable environment for the rest of her life where she'll never have to worry about paying for anything, a difficult adjustment after struggling for so many years to keep us alive.

Embracing the freedom of having enough money to live the way I like and without much effort, I love the challenge and satisfaction of being all kinds of woman for the camera.

Shamen's music inspired those personas. His music was my alter ego. In some way he took possession of me. Like a druggie I needed his music to perform and lost perspective of the mission to investigate him. Yet when he was the first person on Earth to touch me when I came out of the womb, his touch and my awareness of what he represents annexed my soul, maintaining a sliver of consciousness before I realized who he was this time.

The Shamen element influenced me as I dressed to affect him. Like a good chess player, he used me as a pawn. I had no idea he was programming me, hypnotizing me to perform in a way I never thought possible. The cost was precarious and dangerous beyond anything I was prepared for. I was made to receive his gifts of sensitivity and music through pain and humiliation. Knowing what he had done and how I followed I can't lose the anger for falling into his control.

CHAPTER THREE

Descending to the landing zone of Shamen's New Mexico headquarters, the sounds of Franz Liszt' *MEPHISTO WALTZ* comes into my headphones, drowning out the guttural sound of the helicopter as it comes closer to Earth.

A sideways dip exposes teepees and shacks scattered over the green valley of the Sangre de Christo Mountains. Years ago a contingent of Buddhist monks called these mountains one of the eight holiest places on Earth. Testament to that is the contingent of devout groups living quietly and privately among its folds and aprons.

But this delegation is not a spiritual quest. Bernstein and Kalman, my two ex-bosses, have become the *producers* of my wedding. They're here to approve Shamen whose hot, sexy music will put an edge to the frosting on the over-the-top wedding cake of a marriage event. After taking over my first and former client, Tim Jenkins, the counterpart to this wedding as my fiancée, Bernstein and Kalman, otherwise known as BK, will squeeze as much publicity out of our union as possible. As I later learned the marriage had been plotted before my dearly departed makeup man gave me the idea to go to Washington D.C. to experience power. He was not making it up. D.C. was an exciting place to be.

And now this coupling and pending marriage are the perfect ingredients for a star loving public; a movie star handsome State Senator running for the U.S. Senate on his way to the Presidency. His glittering prop, the soon to be beautiful wife who had a superstar career as a model before meeting her political knight in shining armor.

Although I admit to the feel-good I have for my poster perfect fiancée, this was essentially an arranged marriage to which I was one of two principal participants. It guaranteed my financial future. That had been worked out before the public announcement and *the leaked gossip* guaranteed us a strong social awareness. All conceived and expedited in less than a year.

Along with rumors of our pending engagement, I became a target for paparazzi and fashion editorials covering designers I may favor, beauty changes and every accessory I wear or carry. I was offered huge amounts of money to wear designer clothes and even more to show up at various clubs and restaurants. I refused. I'm not a walking billboard and I'm not for sale. I thought.

Because I was caught in the grid of paparazzi and sound bites, I was essentially clueless about my role in this media generated circus. When Tim would not be intimate with me after our first and only time together, I should have seen where this was headed. But I didn't. I gobbled up the promises and acted the part. It was a huge lesson. it took a long time to learn.

But that was then and this is what I'm watching in an experiential way as I time travel out of body. What a gift. I just love the ability to do this.

As the Sangre de Christo mountains come closer and clearer, I look at my former employers, Bernstein and Kalman, and giggle to myself that these overweight and not very attractive men are two of the hottest star making publicists on the planet. BK as they're known in the inner circles can make or break any public entity using twisted information and solid gold connections. With laser precision and speed, they are the most powerful publicists in the world.

In case you don't know my history, I had decided to go to Washington when a makeup artist I worked with told me D.C. can change the world. I wanted to be part of that. My enthusiastic naivete learned quickly that success in Washington is not as easily achieved as New York's fashion world. Highly educated and socially charged people, some with exceptional high IQs or devious low ones, control what is often called the most powerful country on the planet. Powerful or not, D. C. can be a dangerous jungle filled with poisonous traps. One has to move carefully or wake up dead.

My first and only client, Timothy Jenkins, was Bernstein and Kalman's newest five-star attention. With the solid gold potential to make it to the White House and leader of the free world, he came with a heavyweight armory of money and political backing. Tim became my fiancée generating strong publicity to win his party primary and become a candidate for the U.S. Senate from Illinois. He was one of those intense lessons I had to learn on my trek for knowledge.

Before my Washington experience, I was earning a lot of money by looking into a camera or walking down a runway. The perks came from a world that uses icons to satisfy fantasies.

Arriving in DC and landing in the center of the machine that drives public perception gave me the drive to learn as much as possible to reach my personal ideal. I can't explain it because I didn't know what the ideal was. It's a feeling to help to make a difference, a drive that seems to control mind and actions without being obvious. When I talked to my makeup artist, Washington D.C. clicked as a stepping-stone toward making a positive difference in the world. A feeling I hadn't been aware of till that moment - my ah ha moment toward a goal in this life.

The more I learned, the more I wanted to know. A tourist in this political jungle I had no idea when I first got there if I wasn't careful there were lethal traps.

My ideals started to shred after joining the Bernstein and Kalman team. With the glamorous and charming Tim Jenkins as my first client, I broke the promise to myself not to fall in love and gave him my virginity the first night we met.

Immediately because of my glamorous exposure I became the focus of gossip as arm candy and marriage potential for the handsome young politician making a national name for himself. *"Otherwise, why would she be at Bernstein & Kalman"* were the whispers over lunches that would materialize in social media nearly the moment they were uttered.

The fantasy of a life I had posed for had been a dress rehearsal for my new role as the fiancée of an up-and-coming politician. Even my personal classic fashion taste was perfect for that role.

The event to be consummated was designed to be as extravagant and expensive as William and Kate's royal wedding. The international guest list was heavy on the photo opportunity of Hollywood *royalty* which would make Shamen a super star if BK approved him. In retrospect, what Shamen will do with that power is my present concern.

Since mastering the ability to travel back and forth in time, I pretty much know what's going to happen in most situations. However, I don't have the ability to change them. Sometimes I want to, like with Amanda.

But as I had whispered into Amanda's ear, t*he journey is your inner power, the force we search to access it. Signs and guides point the way. It's a question of seeing and accepting them.*

I do my best as a guidepost but I sometimes lose my way. Those of us in training are still controlled by Earth's atmosphere, physically and mentally.

Besides working in a clothing store in high school, my first office job was as the media consultant for BK PR. The position was to use my visual media skills to teach political candidates and their families' techniques for public exposure.

But you may already know the reason behind my hiring if you've been following my career. To put it succinctly, I was set up and screwed, literally and professionally. The lesson as again in so many of my lifetimes, has been to know in any kind of experience there is the choice to be victim or student. And with all the pitfalls I've experienced I still choose *student,* a path of expansion rather than the abyss of victimhood.

Sometimes reality is crushing and victimhood is revealed by those who give up and surrender to be safe. Landing, few moves beyond, the lesson is to hold the goal.

BAM! Stravinsky's *SOLDIER'S TALE* crashes into the *MEPHISTO WALTZ* again, this time on the strings of a very loud, electronic guitar. Ethereal and gritty the sound is perfect for my wedding. I give Bernstein and

Kalman a big smile and thumbs up. Grimacing Bernstein shakes his head, Kalman covers his headphones with his hands.

Ignoring their prejudgments, I point to the open door of the helicopter as we land, visible waves of energy cutting through the morning mist as the approaching copter casts it's shadow over the green valley its landing on. Dust erases the energy lines as the four-pronged ship sends swirls of red dust scattering over the inhabitants of the near-by shacks who had come to see who's landed on their terrain. It's a real-life projection of the future meets the past.

So many signs easy to miss. Hopefully my consciousness has grown sharper and deeper than it's been since the last time I saw my adversary, my lover, in lifetimes before. And now, in this one, he's been my deliverer.

Does Shamen represent my last lifetime on Earth, its last reincarnation? Has he protected me in a way that kept my head above the slime to draw power and strive toward the positive. Escape what Shamen represents.

The steps swing down and our threesome, clothed in varied versions of Japanese black and blue chic, descend the steps to change the energy of the idyllic hippy village in their dusty pastel costumes.

A set designer could not make this place look more factual. Its times like this I revel in the newfound ability to view events as participant and viewer at the same time.

Red dust dulls the silver trim of my wonderful Dries cowboy boots as I pass picture perfect children sitting under a Banyan tree, putting together creative inspirations from found objects.

Watching over the little ones, a young woman with waist long braids turns, bringing an angelic face over a belly so round it looks ready to pop.

"Hi, I'm SUNNY." Her voice is as cute as she looks.

"This is Shamen's baby, but he's not ready to talk yet. He's waiting to be born."

"Well tell him hello for me when he arrives."

We smile. Partners of a feminine kinship.

The muted music I've been hearing suddenly amplifies and crashes our conversation with dissonance.

Looking toward the source Sunny shakes her head when it abruptly stops and smiles. "I guess that means he's coming out." She turns back to the children.

Breath catches in my throat as the real-life version of promotional material comes to life and I'm seeing Shamen in a raw and different way. Shaking long dirty blond hair out of blue eyes so bright they don't seem real, I have no doubt this is the sexiest, most desirable man alive. Young and manly, his looks have a sensitive, sexy, altar boy appeal. Innocent and sexy. What a combination!

But the finely chiseled face doesn't look happy. He isn't hiding his impatience with the interruption and annoyance about a meeting he had accepted days before. He knows Bernstein and Kalman can bring him great success. The gritty country boy hidden in the mountains of New Mexico understands the magnitude of these power brokers who arrived. They can make him a star.

Holding out his hand to shake mine the touch puts me totally back into my body, back to the past which is now the present. Taking clues from this entity called Shamen, I'm surprised how soft his hand is. Holding my hand a little longer than usual, I feel a strange vibration both captivating and a little scary. Not sexy, stimulating. His energy captivated me the first time I felt his hands on me so many lifetimes ago. I can't go back. I have to keep with the present to grow.

Ostensibly this trip is no more than booking music for my wedding. I had to convince the BK boys that this music carried me through much of my career and will be a great asset for the wedding. What I didn't say is this music will offset the commercial fluff of the ceremony with its edginess. I know I'm right. Also I wanted Shamen there for a myriad of reasons. Plus I love his music.

And with the edge I have on Shamen now, I can learn what he wants. There's a reason he materialized in the delivery room to bring me into this reality, then disappeared for two decades till now.

His eyes say he's reading my mind as he shrugs, a chastened, dimpled, schoolboy. "Sorry for the musical tantrum." His smile increases his charm.

Without thought I'm smiling, tingling. He's captivating.

"Your music is exciting, possibly irritating, listeners' choice." A smile is plastered on my face as I say words that won't be removed.

Shamen draws my eyes into his own and the tingling expands. "You've got it. That's why we're here."

His smile is hypnotizing. He's good, but I can block him. I know those smoldering, sexy message types. Models use them all the time.

"Guess I should leave the Masters alone." He breaks the spell and shrugs with a smile as innocent as possible. His charm paints him fascinating. Even though I've seen him before, there is more I want to know.

"Your music is magical," I say with the kind of bright smile that hides what I'm thinking.

"Come see where it's made." He puts out his hand but I ignore it, not wanting him to touch me, not wanting his surging energy into me.

Past a rickety front porch and dilapidated kitchen, Shaman leads us into a gleaming high tech, state of the art, insulated, recording studio that can record and mix anything with top-of-the-line technology.

"A musician's dream," I say.

"Worth a few million," he mumbles.

I wonder where that money comes from, quickly enters my mind.

The instruments start to blur. Beyond the lights of the huge computer mixing board are the shadows of two men deep in conversation.

I float into a new dimension where I am hearing both thoughts and conversations. There is another man with Shamen. I don't think it's Bernstein or Kalman, but I can't tell who it is. I wonder what I'm supposed to see.

I love going places out of sight, but I must remember this is a precious gift to be used for the greater good. I cannot let the tool become the destination.

I will myself back to Shamen and the man I can't see. But I stop myself. I'm hearing words clearly. They're meant for me to hear. In a cool voice Shamen tells the man in no uncertain terms, "I compose alone, kill myself to keep the purity and I'm not going to let some mechanic fuck it up."

"He's a technician, he'll speed your creative efforts, make it happen."

The man could be Kalman, but he's out of my focus and his voice so muffled I can barely hear the words. I'd like to get closer but I'm not sure how much either one knows about my ability and if they have their own. I can't read that yet.

Shamen's sexiness arouses me though I know enough to stay away from him, to not let him get near me in any kind of sexual way. He could destroy me as he has in the past. It is not Shamen I don't trust, it's me. I've been given the techniques to use for the good and I can't lose sight of the goal as I get more involved with my mission.

"Dennis created and built the circuitry on your board," the man was saying. "He knows your music and what you're doing. He's loyal. That's your end of the deal. For us, as before, pay back the favor."

Shamen's eyes grow hard as marble. "Another favor." The statement is flat. No inflection. I try to find a clearer space so I can know what he's hiding.

Flash! A spark flies. I watch with amazement as the man plugs into Shamen with an energy so powerful I can see it. It frightens me a little. Is he tuning him up, activating buttons for behavior?

"This is our second investment," the man is saying. "We gave you the materials, you make the music. Dennis helps, we make you a star. You keep the fame, the fortune and all that goes with it as payment."

Shamen looks straight into the man's hooded eyes, not blinking from the unreal light and energy coming from them. A still frame of master and robot. They bow their heads in agreement as I finish the thought. An accident? A sign?

I'm dealing with something otherworldly that seems to be expanding over Planet Earth and controlling it.

Do I have the tools, the connection to take this on myself? Where are the Voices guiding me through this? I know I have the skills to transport and go to other places to gather information. But it's usually physical, not unspoken intent or secret ruminations. Hopefully the meaning will surface in a way I can understand.

Shamen turns around, winks and smiles. A ripple runs through me as if I'm still on Planet Earth. How long did he know I was in the Ethers? And was that Kalman talking to him? I still can't tell. I had been caught up in reading messages through the physical and only caught the details, not the whole picture.

The two men go to a helicopter that is less significant than the one I will arrive in later. Once the smaller, chunkier man is loaded on to the helicopter, Shamen turns away and pauses, the late morning light cloaking him with a red and golden glow. The colors vibrate, sending a powerful magnetism radiating excitement. Am I reacting to the man who is excited and knows success is near, or is he a robotic implant able to manufacture the energy of excitement and send it to humans?

He does seem to be glowing. He knows the man lifting off in the helicopter will deliver him stardom. Robot or human, Shamen has made a deal with the devil, sold his soul to Lucifer for fame and fortune.

Maybe existence? Can a robot fear dismemberment, of turning into a pile of junk after living as a human on Earth? Is a robot capable of making simple decisions with a power that drives their thought? Do they have feelings?

If that were the case, Shamen could have a soul. He could be a superhuman. Lucifer's end was damnation to Hell. Does Shamen know what he's doing? Does he think he can escape eternity in hell? If he's other earthly or even a robot, there will be no punishment, no hell. Only a metaphoric burial as a bucket of spare parts.

As the helicopter lifts away, I try to come close to Shamen to get what he's feeling. He doesn't allow contact, setting up a wall of total indifference. He knows about astral traveling. He understands me. That's dangerous.

As the helicopter disappears Shamen's smile fades, his marble eyes soften and fill with a flicker of uncertainty, as if he questions what he had just done. Then quickly shakes the thought away and buoyantly goes back to his studio.

He's shown fear. He's human. There was vulnerability. Robots programmed with the highest sophisticated A.I. technology have never to my knowledge, questioned itself or the programmer. The spark reminded him he has made an irreversible choice. That connection says I can reach him and learn how he has been programmed. He knows I see him and chooses a thin, nearly transparent awareness not to acknowledge it. I want to know what he is hiding from me.

The Voices are quiet. What can I do on my own? I'm a little scared without them. Will they help if I need them?

The thought is a roller coaster, and I don't like roller coasters. *Forget the self-doubts and get back on track,* I hear loud and clear. Are the guides back? Then this is a training session. I take a deep breath, a feat with no visible body!

A single Guitar string vibrates. It's incessant, one, two beat sticks in my head and my thoughts change. This is a new beat, a code to guide me, a new level of physical involvement. The voices have changed shape and have become beats in my psyche, a primitive tribal beat that controls thought.

It's the primal pulsing energy that Shamen delivers to hypnotize people and make them his emotional slaves. Am I one as well? Following him as a suspicious investigator, do I want to get closer to him? Once again, can I justify fear by fooling myself with a self-imposed reality?

There is so much to consider – especially when it's required to think of everything at once. So many layers of consciousness swirl around us, waiting to be tapped and entered. Shamen has exposed a dark connection to something that requires objectivity and digging. I wouldn't have been alerted if it wasn't important to understand.

I recognize danger from other connections I've had with men I've loved. Shamen is different. My connection to him is fueled by the need to know who he is. What is he going to do with his power. There is no love now. I no longer allow that good feeling to guide me away from my primary goal to learn what his might be.

Shamen came to me quite unintentionally when I was practicing astral travel. I'd met him a few years before when I was walking a fashion show in Brussels. Captured by his music, excited and inspired, I had become an astral groupie by remote viewing this sexy hunk who intrigued me. Feeling my presence, he was able to bring me in closer. Out of body with little or no resistance he was able to draw me in like a magnet, a puppet melting into his consciousness.

Then when I was about to give myself totally to him, something, a heartbeat, some kind of psychic jerk, yanked me out of this milky comfort to sharp awareness. Once again I was in danger of losing myself to him. Everything I worked so hard to achieve, I would lose and have to be born again.

There is a dark hole in the center of Shamen's spirit. I feel it enticing me though I know there is great danger in whatever is buried there. It could be the heart of a criminal, someone that has no soft edges, no awareness or care about the damage it does.

Using all my might I pull myself out of his energy and slide away. He seems to barely notice and lets me go, uninterested in discovering anything about me. But then, he may already know everything from past life experiences or a program to turn me into a consciousness he controls.

I ask the Guides to take me into the future with Shamen. Perhaps the answer is there.

Closing down my senses the mustiness lifts. I feel safe to breathe and open my eyes. It's the middle of the night and Shamen is hanging out with Dennis, his technician. They've just finished a session.

"Man, I twisted those amps to balance your vision of coming to light till my wrists nearly contracted." Dennis shook out his hand and grabbed a beer bottle. "We got it. The contradiction of heavy metal and ethereal light. It's so cool."

Shamen clinks his bottle against Dennis's. When I married Tim, the wedding guests had been blown away by Shamen's music. At the time I paid little attention because I was focused on not showing the panic I was feeling as I acted the part of the happy bride. At that time, I had only just begun to learn how to focus and go out of body to other dimensions. I used it in front of the camera when I became different characters and let my body react to what

I was feeling. Like a character in Frank Herbert's book, "*Dune*", I would become a face dancer. Shamen can do that too.

In retrospect there had been obvious messages that could have saved me a lot of pain. Not paying attention it took me longer to find the ability to defy gravity and three-dimensional space. It's only recently I've been able to achieve travel undetected through time. It's all about directing the mind and using the positive end of the struggle to dominate and turn it to light. It's a great high. I hope to live in it once I evolve.

Guess that's why I'm writing this present account with Shamen, not knowing if it's really the last one but it has more clarity than other lifetimes before. The lesson is to keep the lesson going. Diversion throws shadow on the goal toward light.

I float behind Shamen into his studio. If he knows I'm here, he shows no sign of it. His focus is solely on Dennis.

"Dennis, you're so sensitive to my voice. The instruments are a vocal, coming from our hearts." Shamen's excitement is contagious. They clink their bottles again. "This is fucking great."

"The album is brilliant," Dennis adds. "The critics will love it."

"Yeah," Shamen grins, his dimples cutting a perfect frame for his slightly pouty lips. "They have good taste."

Sunny comes through the door. Back lit by the outdoor lights her newly thin and toned body is revealed beneath a nearly transparent spun silk caftan.

"It's late, why don't you come to bed?" Coming close to Shamen, her bare leg reaches out to rub his as her hand travels up his thigh.

He holds her hand in place and turns to Dennis.

Pulling away Sunny asks, "will it make you happy to bring him along?"

Shamen turns to Dennis.

"Do you want to sleep with her?"

"I'd like nothing better. You won't mind?"

Shamen shrugs noncommittedly. "Not if Sunny doesn't. What do you say Darling? Shall we share our love with the man who's helping to make this music happen?"

She turns to leave. "Why me? You have each other." In a flurry of sheer silk Sunny leaves the studio.

Shamen and Dennis turn back to their instruments and start a riff, their bodies fade into wavelengths as they dissolve and reemerge in the green room of a network studio as the riff ends.

I've never so totally melted into the out of body energy of a person I'm viewing. Is this my own doing or is Shamen or some entity controlling this split screen movie I'm seeing as my life. I can't tell the specific date or time on a search for signage. An identifying cap or sweatshirt to tell me where I'm at or what year would do.

I just know when I get caught in Shamen's energy, I'm pulled beyond the third and fourth dimensions where I can no longer hold on to Earth. It's frightening because I'm not sure I can return. Like being in a runaway car with no brakes, no stability, no gravity. And yet, when directed, it provides the most incredible journey I had never dreamed to have.

There is so much to learn but fear holds me back. I can't leave this life till my senses are mastered and I'm not afraid to leave. That is when I believe my evolution will continue. I just want to stay conscious on the way.

Grabbing a breath, I stand back from the vision of Shamen, the pampered prince. Stretched out in a tall director's chair, hands clasped behind his perfectly layered platinum-blond hair, he shuts his eyes as the makeup artist paints a dark Egyptian slant on his lids. He opens them to look at me.

Not sure if it's the makeup with its phosphorescent mauve and silver eye shadow or Shamen has an unworldly glow. Tucked into tight silver jeans that seem to quiver with their carefully sewn silver threads, his image is sexy, cool and casual.

Surrounded by an adoring entourage of cheap and chic, I recognize some, but don't know why. Spotting Shamen's brother Michael, I go to him. Sweet and innocent, dressed in immaculate yoga whites, he is Shamen's go-fer. He doesn't see me or sense my presence. True, I'm not in the flesh nor did I know I was going forward in time. Am I to change something? We can't change destiny. Who makes the rules?

Michael gets closer, unaware he is nearly covering Shamen now. People in the room are calling him Sadhu. But Sadhus are usually older men who give up their material world to go into the wilderness to live hand to mouth. Michael, or Sadhu doesn't seem to be giving up worldly assets. He is a free spirit and probably got his new name because he's the group pet, always there when someone needs something. Everyone loves him. He's exactly the image Shamen likes to convey.

Sunny comes into the room, totally changing my first impression of her the day we met in the mountains. Her naturally curly hair is flat ironed straight and silky and she wears a chic but funky Yohji Yhamamoto *don't give a damn outfit* that costs a lot more than it appears.

Planting a kiss on Shamen's cheek he pulls away. "You smell of alcohol. Where's Raja?"

"A four-month old's company gets tiresome. Try it sometime."

"You're handing my kid off to anyone who passes by. He's never with you anymore."

"Why don't you try taking care of him? Your followers would be honored to change his diaper for you." Turning to leave she pauses, "Raja is napping. Sadhu is watching him."

"Maybe you should start watching Raja instead of putting that stuff up your nose. I've got to get ready. I need to be alone."

"You're always alone," she tossed back as she walked away, holding on to her flimsy dignity, determined not to let Shamen see the hurt and anger she felt.

I'm not sure of the time-line – it could have been five months or five years into the future – I can't determine the difference. But when I first met Sunny she looked like an angel. Now she's pretty but molded, a mannequin of her initial fresh innocence.

From what I'm observing from this perch in the ethers, Shamen has cut off from everyone around him. Maybe that's why Sonny's demeanor is so different from what she used to be. The love and closeness they shared seems vanished.

Is my quest to find this man's secret motivated by a desire to hang him for his past deeds? Do I want retribution, revenge or is my intention pure? Many lessons come to me through the experiences of others.

Dark clouds gather and swirl around Shamen as he leaves the dressing room, mumbling he was going to the can. I follow as he leaves the theatre through a side entrance and walks through one of the narrow alleyways that separate this theatre from another. Keeping a few feet overhead in the gloomy night, he's looks like a creepy animation from one of the theatre posters lining the walls, his black ankle length trench coat swishing and swirling around his every step.

However, his energy isn't lighthearted or comic. A buzzing surrounds the figure like a nest of hornets, a cloud of darkness descends and covers him as he leaves the alleyway to approach a family of three. I hear a low pop, the woman slumps to the ground, the young girl screams, "Mommy!", the older man starts to chase the assailant then stops and goes back to his wife and daughter as the trench coated man disappears in the pre-show crowds.

A musician turns up the volume on his phone. "Hey, listen to this. Ellen Baxter, Senator Stuart Baxter's wife just got shot."

"Ewww that's horrible. Weren't they supposed to come to the concert tonight? I was arranging a photo op with the Senator and ... oh my god, it could have been one of us.

Shamen's head snaps up. "We've been here for hours."

"She was popular," says Ralph Whitehead, the road manager. "But there was a lot of anger at the Senator."

"Is she dead?" asks the makeup artist, gluing rhinestones across Shamen's head like a browband.

"People shot in the head usually die," Shamen growls uncharacteristically.

"She was shot in the head?" asks Ralph.

I feel the chill from Shamen's cold response as he turns and looks at me, challenging, smiling, ignoring Ralph.

I stay quiet, recreating that moment on the New York Street. In the snow it had become a black and white film. Was it real? Does Shamen know what I think I saw?

"This is a big deal," Ralph keeps talking. "She was beautiful and popular, known for her charity work especially for underprivileged children and the homeless. Since her documentary on undocumented children taken from their families and put in cages, she's been in the national spotlight, promoting the fact hundreds are still separated and lost in the system. Her killing is a targeted message".

The young girl on the drummer's lap scrolls down her phone. "Her teenage daughter Kelsey was next to her when she got shot. Eww, can you imagine." She continues to scroll. "Senator Baxter got the tickets along with backstage passes as a gift for Kelsey's sixteenth birthday.

"Shit." Ralph stiffens. "This is going to screw the concert."

A bulletin flashes on the huge video screen. The assailant has been found. There is a murmured sound of relief. Shamen smiles.

A chill comes through me. Shamen is the one who shot Ellen Baxter then walked away from a beloved wife, a loving mother, and a woman who shared her goodness so others could have better lives. Dead.

Now, probably a drifter or homeless person is going to be charged with her murder. How can I accuse Shamen? I've been out of body the whole time. No one would believe me without solid proof.

If I tried, I'd have to reveal my fourth-dimension abilities and few would believe that. My credibility and mission would be destroyed. I can't tamper with destiny. It's irrefutable, it can't be changed. Only our perception, the takeaway is what matters in the universal scheme of existence.

A worried looking production assistant comes walking in fast. "The audience isn't responsive to the warm-up. They're distracted and some are walking out. Sorry about this but I thought you should know."

"Thanks Shelley."

Shamen smiles, a praying Mantis rubbing his hands he calls his group together.

"This is our first international streaming across the planet. It's been hyped for months as the best event ever. Our music is already a household name and tonight we put our purest energy to it."

"But people are distracted and upset," interrupted the young production assistant, cheeks wet with tears, forgetting backstage protocol not to question Shamen.

"What we want," Shamen smiles broadly and takes the young assistant's hand and pats it, "is to raise them up with our magic, our music. Soothe and comfort them with love."

He uses his melodic primal beat to affect his team the way he manipulates audiences and also me. Radiating comfort and excitement in an electronic way the energy of the sound affects how people hear it. Spoken or sung it has an unconscious yet familiar beat that manipulates our feelings. He uses the technique to capacity whenever the situation warrants it. If ever he needed to use it, it's tonight.

"Ready for success" Shamen preaches to the band and the entourage. "Our music will knock the tragedy out of their minds and put us in the hearts of a star-seeking, Messiah hungry public. We'll supply the means for transference. They will love us because we make them feel good and make them forget the horror of what has happened outside these doors."

In unison, the band transforms from concern to excitement as they get ready to go on stage. Imbued with purpose they will achieve public transformation because Shamen has given them the gift of purpose to empower their performance as they live stream to the world their first time ever.

Floating through the audience I see publicists, managers, and agents I've known from past lifetimes, not wondering till later how they all assembled from the past. At the moment it's exciting not to be seen as I watch the audience react.

The well-programmed word of mouth about Shamen is working. Almost no one has seen him perform which makes him more desirable. The millions poured into his campaign seem to be paying off for this live stream.

Suddenly the theatre and the thousands of social media screens throughout the world go dark. With a flash I almost miss, Shamen's appearance on stage is in a blaze of light. Screams of the groupies paid to stand by the stage and shriek their love gets the audience to do the same.

Dressed in those custom silver jeans hugging his long powerful legs, Shamen, with the physique of a dancer, strides to the edge of the stage. His glistening white-blonde hair is heightened with key lights framing his head like a halo. Hands clasped piously at his waist he is a plugged-in solid-state icon.

"He's so hot," gushes a young girl, struggling to join the paid groupies at the foot of the stage.

"God I love him," squeals another young thing spaced out on a designer drug someone handed her.

Bathed in light, surrounded by total blackness, a vision of beauty and virtue Shamen lives up to his well-paid media saturation. Physically projecting any image his brain commands, his plastic ability mesmerizes the audience in the theatre and the millions watching on their preferred devices as a lens zooms in to mesmerize most who watch him.

I recognize so many things he did to me in our past lives which make me sure he was involved in the high-profile deaths that have been occurring across America where he happens to perform. Usually they're local rather than national news. This one has a political backstory that won't go away. It's political and sensational.

Once again I think it possible Shamen is an otherworldly, top of the line, A.I. hitman that freezes human senses into a semi-hypnotic state while he does whatever he wants to intended victims. Trusting in every person there is good, I hang on to the hope if Shamen is human there is *a chance* he can be diverted from doing harm. That's what I have to find out. Truth doesn't lie. It can hide but it ultimately reveals itself.

Pausing for a moment Shamen gestures to the oblivious screaming groupies to stop. As if he waved a wand, silence was immediate and Shamen continued. "You know it could have been one of you. Some crazy walks down the street and shoots someone at random. You never know. There are bad people waiting around the corner to take you away from everything you love. That is what this man has done to Ellen Baxter, leaving her husband Senator Baxter and their daughter Kelsey who was to celebrate her sixteenth birthday with us tonight.

Murmured sounds underscore his sad words.

"We will celebrate their lives by bringing our energies together and send the family so much love they will feel it in their hearts. There is a higher reason for everything that happens and art or tragedy can offer understanding. Knowledge and experience will bring peace."

The audience is silent, waiting for Shamen to lead them. To tell them how to feel. Like a revivalist, Shamen glides into the silence with a soft crooning rendition of Happy Birthday to Kelsey. Caressing the strings of his guitar tears welling in his eyes the cameras move to swooning fans, singing and swaying to this familiar song, forging a bond to each other and to the man leading them to feel this way.

Amazing Grace comes in for a few bars then the Crooner segues into four words; *JUSTICE, TRUTH, LIGHT, FORGIVENESS* as the words flash on the wall behind; JUSTICE, TRUTH, LIGHT, FORGIVENESS.

Ending with hot classic rock percussion, turning Shamen's simple yet sexy looks into a heart-grabbing presence for an audience seeking diversion from the realities of the night.

In a multilevel way I simultaneously see the present and future and feel the moment the public transfers it's feelings from grief to comfort. Shamen became the touchstone, their Idol, a superstar with easy words that resonate.

Already responsive to Shamen through the brilliant worldwide campaign by Bernstein and Kalman, Shamen was a star before he came on the stage. It would seem his marketing impact would be challenged by the brazen murder of Ellen Baxter. Instead, the public is ready to buy everything Shamen gives them. His simple and quiet commercial sounds engage the public. They feel stronger and better because of him and for that reason he becomes their instant hero, their superstar.

With the power of the public behind him, I'm not sure why I am so closely aligned with him. I had been on a clear and smooth road to my destination and once again I'm stopped, sidelined by his needs while ignoring my own.

Searching my emotional data base, I am convinced there is nothing personal or sexual about this man I seem to be stalking, both in and out of body. I recognize too many shadows signaling me to keep emotionally alert and away from personal feelings. He could be a honey trap, like the undercover agents who posed as prostitutes in WWII to get information from the Nazi high command. I don't think I have anything to give him, and I have to stop thinking about his behavior and follow my instincts to do what I can in this individual infinite way.

Shamen's first album sold out long before his first live stream. Social media companies lined up with barrels of cash and goodies for his endorsement. The few he initially took to tantalize future endorsements earned him millions of dollars along with countless more fans.

Agents controlling Shamen's business priced him so high that he became news in the financial market. With millions of dollars in various currencies, stables of cars, horses, exotic animals and aircraft, Shamen's first year in the entertainment world is the biggest in rock star history.

After the murder of the Senator's wife, Shamen's poster, a luminescent tear on the rim of his eye, becomes a valuable collector's item. His rise as an international household name, is so fast I wait for NASA to name a comet, SHAMEN .

I try to use my newfound abilities to locate a chink in Shamen's armor, but he appears to be squeaky clean. Maybe more perfect than a human.

Then there is the hooded man in the long coat who killed Ellen Baxter. Was it Shamen or do I want it to be him? Is this incarnation of Shamen the same entity that had meant so much to me in so many past lifetimes? I sense and have a flash awareness of the terrible things he had done to me. I see who he is. However, the question remains, is he human, an A.I. robot, or a species from another planet? Most important, why is he here?

He knows I'm using remote viewing and transporting out of body, but he doesn't seem to care. Though aware of my presence he won't acknowledge it. Hide and Go Seek on an astral plain. However, in the three-dimensional world, did he know what I was or was I only the conduit to the best mass marketing on the planet?

CHAPTER FOUR

Where he'll stop, who knows. Every time I see Shamen I know how dangerous he can be. Yet the challenge to reach him, lighten his perceptions, guide him toward light is irresistible.

When I think of giving Shamen light, I vividly remember the bright light nearly searing my eyes as I'm tied to a chair, my head pulled back and secured with some kind of metal structure I couldn't see.

I wasn't seeing much. I was frozen – inside and out. Terror was like an icy blanket holding me down. Yet it gave me a mental structure to see out and not let anyone know there was someone inside.

The handsome Officer in the uniform of the Third Reich pulled me from the chair and whirled me around and around, pulling me up as I collapsed from exhaustion. Holding a small gold bullet shaped object with holes like a saltshaker at the top, he shoved it under my nose and I involuntarily inhaled. Energy back I continued to turn like a rat on a treadmill till dizziness made colors go black.

Stiff and leaning against a large tank with a huge alligator inside, a sharp slap whipped my head back and I flew out to the Universe, flying through stars and planets, searching for the planet where I lived. I want to go home.

But a sharp object under my throat starts cutting the front of my silk dress shoving me back into awareness of the metal chair, the tight leather ropes around my arms, my neck and head pulled back. I can't see the Officer drawing the knife blade down my throat, slitting my silk dress down the front, ripping it open.

Rough hands pull my sliced bra off my body and I sit, legs spread and secured. My arms tied to the sides of the metal chair and my head secured so tightly I can't move. I can't breathe either. Everything has welled up. My eyes are wide open, but I'm too scared to see.

A grey-white cloud lifts me up and takes me away. I look down and see myself and it makes me sad. I want to go back and comfort the poor girl in the chair. Then I see the man standing in front of her, arms crossed, deciding what to do.

I want to help her, but the knowledge of what it will cost in terms of her self-help is too high. I close my eyes and feel soft but strong hands on my naked flesh. He had pulled up the skirt of my dress and ripped my stockings down from my thighs where they now gather at my ankles. I'm mortified. I don't know what to do and will myself back into the ethers, into the gray-white mass, away from the body going through such agony.

Hours, maybe days, I've lost all sense of time, I'm naked on the cement floor of a tiny cell, closed off to all light. My body aches, every limb, muscle, patch of bruised flesh is a package of pain. Maybe I've fallen down a flight of cement steps, then I remember the sexual attack then nothing.

I summon the clouds to come and take me away, but they don't. I hear a familiar voice telling me to *keep breathing and stay calm. Don't relate to what they are doing. They have their own agenda; you don't have to follow if you don't want.*

The officer looks into my eyes. His eyes are unearthly blue and compelling. I feel like I'm falling into them.

"Don't! Pull back" screams in my head. *"Don't get dragged into his head. He's a robot. He's not from here and if you let down he will take you. You'll lose your objectivity; he's done it to you before. He's otherworldly, unearthly, his energy is compelling because he's programed to get you this way. His technology is unearthly. He can make you perform in ways you'd never dream of – and he does this without a word."* The words chill me. They're coming from the place of trust.

These are the words that become thoughts manifesting into ideas that change my life. They give me the understanding that takes care of me.

Carl Jung, the founder of analytical psychology says our *Instincts* are linked to our highest selves. The higher realms of awareness. Instincts and creativity, tickets for an Angel Express.

Snap! Maybe I can find out if Shamen is a manufactured human from an A.I. construction that simulates emotion and sensitivity. I thought he was human when he turned away from the helicopter after selling his soul, but then recently, from what I have observed he may be a manufactured being that looks and acts and appears to think like a human, but he's not. He knew I was watching him. His type is very smart, and they sometimes fool me when I allow a coated version of the benefit of the doubt. Not this time. The stakes are too high. I'm betting on light.

The experiences I had with Shamen in different centuries when no technology of this sophistication existed, meant that he could have been controlled by some kind of power that can change the energy of feelings. Evolution turned these physical means of connecting into aspects of ourselves driven by technology. Good drama can elicit tears or laughter. A sophisticated telescope can take you to the stars. A tab of a plant or a tiny pill can reveal secrets of the Universe within or outside the body.

"It's important to learn to take control of consciousness", says that voice whose beliefs I take as my own. *"Leaving your body must never be done without positive consent."*

Hope I remember most of this so if I get out alive, I can write it down. I'll call it fiction, so I don't have to defend my belief that people know what they're capable of but sometimes afraid to trust it. For the moment, I have no air in this cement box. I can barely move. How can people do this to others?

The officer in charge is Shamen. I knew it from the deep unease I felt when he came close to me. Once again his steely coldness rippled down my back, shutting down my lungs, literally taking my breath away. In other more innocent lives those feelings were exciting. Made me aware of new places new triggers in my body that made me feel different. When I met Shamen in those lives, he set off those good feelings.

He put his hand on my shoulder and the familiar shock waves were sent. Not frightening or pleasurable, only a jolt of power, a signpost. It doesn't matter, it's all the same. We're part of an endless Universe that can possess power on the tip of a needle.

Going backward and forward in time, I'm learning every message is essentially the same. Somehow there is going to be a block in the journey. The way around is to go through it, no matter what. As the Russian playwright, Chekhov said, *the journey is the destination.*

Perhaps humanity is programmed to allow a pre-determined destiny to take over. Shamen could be a prototype that allows people to make choices. They look no different than they did in the past, yet their vision and minds are controlled by imbedded emotional triggers impelling them to obey.

I underestimated Shamen.

I perceived throughout so many reincarnations that he was trying to control me. In this one I learn I'm a single soul within the Universe brimming with need to connect with light. Shamen is a test along the way.

Again life follows art. It appears Earth is being led to a dependent consciousness. Unable to make independent choices for themselves, spontaneity and freedom will be deemed against the good of the whole. Behaving or even thinking against the regime won't be allowed. The era of the Thought Police trained to read minds and separate words are explicitly designed to cause unrest.

The danger is because the Universe is created to run on the creative, oppression of freedom, a by-product of creativity, will cause unrest.

Shamen's power might be too awful for the populace to contemplate if they feel incomplete without being told how to think and feel. Yet some are aware of that tiny roiling of restlessness generated by the suppression of their creativity and freedom. The inability to no longer be able to think for oneself, to live without independence and freedom is unacceptable.

If Shamen is an A.I. programed robot, who is the person writing his program and how many others like him have been put on Planet Earth? Has the Solid State Conspiracy taken over Earth without a single shot, without our awareness? Will Earth survive?

This might be the closing to the end of the human race through its consciousness. The robots have none.

Discipline and thought is getting too difficult for the population to contemplate because they are being told not to think and react only when told.

But maybe impatience keeps me from seeing the future as bright. Many people are putting resistance to having a pre-determined mind-set and block the doubts that blur thought.

CHAPTER FIVE

Getting my breath back to normal, I'm on Earth in full body, aware of the change in my thinking patterns. I may have to prepare myself for passage from here but I'm too scared and cold to think about my future. For now I want to survive the present on Planet Earth.

I had done plenty of thinking before I had decided to come back to live with the sensibility of three-dimensions. I almost forgot everything is touched by energy that passes by and through each other making us all, in some way, connected. That connection is more weighted than the one I use to reach my dream's summit.

Coming back to Earth after a hiatus in the ethers I dress like a chic young woman radiating light. My costume is a stretchy white jumpsuit, yellow workman ankle boots with two-inch thick rubber soles and sharpened steel toes. My long hair is pushed into a white baseball cap that has been wired for sound. As a personal joke, printed above the rim is, *WIRED*. Actually, I am pretty wired. Being an Earthling makes me vulnerable to physical feelings that make my heart pound and my breathing shallow and fast. I also feel things differently than I do when watching from OOB – out of body, where I don't react to the physical manifestations of Earth.

Like now, shaking convulsively being naked in a closed metal box, it seems the cold and fear are fighting for dominance which makes it worse. There is not a spec of comfort. They have taken my clothes and shaved my head. It's crushing, debilitating. The clothes were ruined and have to be replaced, but my hair will take time I may not have.

Even knowing the Nazi psychological reasoning to take all comfort zones away by keeping captives empty and broken, stripped to the core, they search for strains of vulnerability which I will not show them. They won't destroy my defiance which they'll try to suppress with psychology and physical strength. If I give them that appearance, they'll believe I've been destroyed. But they can't take my consciousness. It's who and what I am, seen or not. They can't possess me as much as they try. They will fail.

Meanwhile if I leave the body encasing who I am, it will be on my terms – not theirs. A last-minute grip of fear will not end my succession to the Universe I aspire to live in. What I don't understand and what I may be here to learn, is the compelling force to keep my life on this planet, when I know so well the freedom of the other dimensions.

Earth tries to convince us another energy doesn't exist. Earth's energy is the only one. But those who experience the other dimensions know them. It's something to be achieved and not easily won. It is probably the reason I'm being forced to experience physical torture without objectivity. The pain and brutality are intense. It's debilitating to be freezing and hear others cry for help, for their Mamas, for their God.

The pleading, and prayers stopped by multiple gun fire is horrifying. In less than a minute poets and scholars, parents and babies, generations of human lives are sadistically lost. I pray their souls escape to the heavens on the words of their prayers, good deeds and beliefs.

Sometimes a few screams escape through the barrage but are quickly stopped by fellow citizens in uniforms willing to kill innocent people who may have been their neighbor or friend in an earlier time.

Given a uniform and an ideal not allowed to be reversed, they react without thought, aiming and pulling a trigger of death, taking a life, someone's love, their reason for being, the potential to change the world with knowledge or talent, are taken out with deadly precision and no hesitation. No thought about what they were destroying and the centuries of rehabilitation these massacres will exact.

Why is there a choice to follow that dark path when its scientifically proven dark cannot win, light erases dark.

Sometimes when I'm weighted with Earth consciousness and murky memories, I forget in another life I had been given the sensation to fly and not be bound by gravity or misconceptions of what can't be done. The big test is to keep the consciousness of being off the Earth while living on it.

At this particular moment, I've got to get the hell out of this mess and gain my freedom to choose another part of my journey. I want to make sure the story is told the way I believe it to be. I don't want to go down as a martyr.

I remember evil well enough to try never to cement my feet to the Earth. The feelings of terror are horrible. My way to deal with it has been to lift away from the reality and refuse to be brought down. Disassociation is a good starting point.

The problem right now is *practicing what I preach*. The box is being opened and I'm being brought out into the open. Its freezing and I'm naked. I curl myself as much as possible from the cold and the shame of my naked body so exposed. I hear a voice saying; *don't feel shame.* I know it's not my fault I tell myself, but I feel it anyway. No one has ever seen me naked or so filthy. I can't look at anyone. If I keep my eyes closed, they won't exist. I have to get away from this. The degradation is almost too powerful. When I give in, it's gelatinous feeling wraps me up like a coiling snake, smothering hope. I become

Amanda, trapped with fear. I know better but I can't control these feelings. I don't know how to get Amanda out of me.

Suddenly I'm suspended over myself watching the Officer, who I know is Shamen, lead me toward a car where he tenderly puts a blanket over my naked shoulders and helps me into the back seat, then follows as well. Beyond this bizarre picture I'm feeling the comfort of familiarity. Also, I'm treasuring the comfort and the softness Shamen gives me.

Basking in these shards of good feeling I'm afraid to look around. The homes are familiar but the people in them or on the road are not the ones I remember. They're all strangers. Even the inactivity; a thick silence under the usual sounds of traffic and talk. No children playing, no dogs barking, not even a horn. It's as if the area is two dimensional and I'm here alone, surrounded by a screen depicting the quiet idyllic scenes of small-town childhood. The screen goes dark and I'm alone with Shamen. Nothing else exists except electric energy surrounding us. I go willingly, a dog following a master to elicit a scrap of kindness, fearful of doing anything wrong.

He opens the door to a beautifully furnished home and I follow. Without looking at me he gestures toward the bathroom.

"Wash off that filth. I want to see the Jewess inside."

Dismissed. A piece of property. A spoil of war. He is going to decide what to do with me. I'm so ashamed of my nudity I cringe as I slide past him to get to the bathroom. The voice inside is telling me to *walk tall. Do not let him see shame. Don't hide.* I hold my breath and close my eyes and will myself, out of body.

"*Stay, change the energy.*" The voices demand.

Weakened by cold and fear, the warm water is making me feel better, but I can't escape. If I run when I get out, where can I go? I have no clothes, nothing to defend myself! I desperately want to leave my body but I'm being held back to accept the process and then go beyond it.

Right now, I'm too scared to calm down and engulf myself in peace and harmony. My body and emotions have taken a life separate from my deepest thoughts and are in control. I hear movement and ignore it to have a few seconds longer in the water, a silvery shield protecting me with the most peace I've had in weeks. Then it's gone. As soon as I'm calmed the water is shut off by Shamen who has opened the door to the glass room and allowed the cold to quickly evaporate the luscious steam that had encased me. Protection is gone.

Shamen motions me to take a few steps forward then dries me off as he would a child. Once again, from lifetimes before, my mind separates from my body and sends me to a low level where I'm a helpless child experiencing these feelings for the first time. Watching my body betray me I open to his painful brutality.

Screaming to push the pain out of my body his grip tightens and as I beg him to stop he slaps me, growling "keep quiet or die." Terror shoots through my body as he manipulates me, knowing from many lifetimes, where to touch me, how to make me give in and open to an intense moment of rapture then pain. The walls of my uterus move on an impulse all their own, grasping and pulling him inside, sensation blocking thought, a new reality.

With that semblance of comfort I'm calmed till Shamen pushes me backward on the bed, an iron-like fist holding my arms over my head. My only focus is his hand and how helpless I am. As much as I try, I can't leave my body. I have no control. To be a pawn in the hand of someone with no caring or connection to humanity is terrifying.

Though I have centuries of wisdom, my mind is blank, I can't connect to even a semblance of comfort I once owned.

Shamen reads my thoughts and emotion. Survival looks bleak. If he wants my soul, he'll never have it. It belongs to the Universe. It's totally unique.

Shamen is moving down my body, his hands pushing my thighs apart, his face coming between my legs and grasping my most secret place in my body with his teeth. Pain tears through me, sending me into screams.

Kicking and pushing against him with my feet, he gets stronger, biting and licking where no one has ever touched before. Gnawing and biting, licking, and grunting, mews of tenderness than a moment stops, arches back then slams into me again and again, not stopping till I'm gratefully allowed out of my body to hover over the moans coming from the figure on the bed as breath whooshes out, a strangled sound of screams turning to moans. Drawn back into my body I'm pounded with pain, moving with his tongue to protect myself from being destroyed.

An errant child, without permission, my body responds to what I don't want to feel. I have no control as my hips lift and my legs widen, the silky warm object plunging, beyond pain, melting a hormonal glacier that in some mystical way says, from this moment my mind and body will never be the same.

I stop struggling and lay compliant as he plunges again and again. Survival may be only 50/50 but I'm flying, separating from this Earthbound rape. As I begin to glory in the power I have back, I plunge back down and find myself looking up at a monster. Hating him for what he's doing and hating myself for responding. My body now an alien separating me from my way to live has taken control of my actions. My purpose now to be a pawn in an Earthbound set of survival chess.

I'm angry for losing the ability to stay out of body and failing this test so badly. What can I do? Stay and get him to use me till I know the truth of his mission? Can my physical body survive this, or even his touch?

His tentacles are long and strong and he can control much of what I do if I confront him. Not knowing if he's superhuman or a new form of robot that can engage with the *flesh carriers;* as the AI Robots call humans, they believe they're superior to us. But they don't know how to initiate a new thought. They can only replicate data. Humans initiate data through detailed work and inspiration.

Shamen can inhabit our senses, make us his pawns because he uses data to inhabit those places. As a programmed personality however, he cannot initiate original thought from the vast input of information put into him.

These Artificial Intelligence Robots seem to have sexy, sensual feelings and are programmed to satisfy a human's most basic, primal needs, the human desire for sensual awareness. Extraterrestrials and Robots want to occupy that as well, but they don't recognize *awareness* since they don't know what it is. They're good at imitation, looking and sounding convincing, but they have only a top layer. There is nothing, no soul, no connection to the creative or anything other than the self. They are programmed for technique. They know how to deal on a current level that humans can only try to emulate. Since both humans and A.I. beings have contrasting goals, the Superhuman has been developed that has equal elements of both. Powered with an A.I. chip this Superhuman is undetectable. Cloaked in beauty with a luscious personality Shamen is an object of perfection difficult to ignore.

Actually I have no idea if he's real or an A.I. entity, but I want to understand my connection with him over so many lifetimes.

Long ago in the life map of my existence, I met Shamen in magical circumstances. Living like a princess, everything going my way, my world is turned upside down when I'm buried in an avalanche. At first I thought Shamen was a hallucination when he appeared through a crack in the tons of ice and snow surrounding me.

A team of rescuers followed him and transported me to a hospital in Germany where they assumed I was never going to be conscious again. Hours before my organs were to be removed, a doctor saw tears in my eyes, the machines keeping me alive had been turned off and I was breathing on my own. My brain function registered normal, actually a little above. In days I was able to talk a bit and walk with a cane.

Shamen had saved me from that avalanche. Now he rapes me.

Transported to a platform in space I see everything happening. Emotionally removed, I'm essentially two persons split in half, the opposite sides of the brain independent of the other. Somewhere in a little spot behind the two halves of my consciousness is the score keeper making judgements and dealing out prizes and punishment.

Shamen's eyes zoom into me. They are primitive, animalistic. The eyes of a wolf.

Bowing to him, the Earth-bound part of me, gets on my knees in between his spread legs. Holding my head to inhale his manliness it reaches to the platform where I feel the energy of the scent hit the center of my body and radiate up to vibrate in my heart. It rises to my throat as I breathe in his essence as the girl on Earth drinks from him. Do I experience the same off Earth as I kneel on Earth as a supplicant?

I close my eyes and the hard floor under my bare knees sends chills up my legs. My shaved head is being held by this potential replica of a human being.

He pulls me away. His penis is erect. He picks me up and puts me on the bed face down.

Putting his hand between my legs he pulls my thighs apart. My heart sinks as they spread. I have no will to fight. I can't win. I close my eyes and ask to go out of body. Face down, legs opened, the penis plunging into me, penetrating my flesh, searing, screaming, burning, he doesn't stop. Pushing and plunging, again and again.

In a frenzy of pain I jump into space. A button has been pushed and *voila* - I'm different. Wet between my legs. I push away from the sleeping man who raped me so I can clean the blood off my legs. I look for any clothes. Used as a naked object is excruciating and the only thing keeping me from exploding is knowing I must find a way to escape. Why am I being blocked? What is the lesson I should learn from this? What should I do to get my power back?

In the refreshing clean shower with hot steamy water and soft fragrant soap I almost feel whole again. Cherishing each drop of water, the soap soothes my very sad skin, makes me feel like the girl – woman I once, not long ago, had been.

The rape changed me. I'll never be the same. Is it part of my education toward what I'm going toward? Or is it just part of the human drama that everyone lives in their own way?

It's not for you to question, came into my mind. *Just live your life in the space of your mind.*

Looking around at the people on the street and at tables near the place I sit alone, I wonder how I got here and how long I have been at this sidewalk cafe.

So much has happened – but has it really? Was it something I had made up while I sit here, waiting for time to pass, waiting for something to happen so I can complete a phase of my journey and continue on to the next?

Time. How much has passed? Where have I been before this café in Paris writing notes to myself? I know what my head has been telling me what to do with the notes once they're down. They say there is a message and a warning and I should get them out. Another side road off the path I had thought was going to be straighter once I knew what awaits me.

Keep going, you'll see, came a directive from my voice of trust.

The tunnel is growing shorter, a dim light at the end of the tunnel is starting to glow brighter. The energy for my body leaves and I become all thought. It's kind of scary to think about floating in the Universe needing only the power to think and create a picture of ourselves for others when needed. And what if we're needed and return to Earth, will we have feet to walk on or are we invisible beings emitting flashes of energy that make others believe we're as real as we think we are? A new class of robot, ASIH – artificial super intelligent human. The bigger question is who is building and programming them?

I have to be careful. I see the thought police looking my way. I know they exist; I've been warned. Dressed in 1930's villain style costumes of black leather coats and wide brimmed hats shading their eyes, they are so cliché I would have laughed had I not feared their danger.

Surrounding me, each crushing an elbow to lift me off the ground and deposit me in the back seat of a car between them and behind a driver I hadn't noticed. I doubt anyone on the street saw what just happened or chose not to.

A blindfold is put over my eyes and my hands and legs are bound with leather restraints.

I close my eyes and ask to leave my body. My heart is beating so hard I fight to take needed breaths. My teeth actually chatter with fear, knowing the next few hours or days will be hell unless I can get myself into the state where I can leave Earth and maintain my consciousness. I know what's coming. It just happened. Do I have to go through it again?

The thought, a kernel size energy controlling all I know and feel at any moment, is too much to accept. I still count on the functioning of the organs of the Earth body to keep the mind sharp. In the mirror the eyes stay the same. They don't lie, they reveal who I am.

Remembering again the degradation and disbelief when the Officer stripped off my clothes in front of his soldiers and forced me to do humiliating things to each one. Yelling and drinking, it became a contest to see who would come the fastest in me. If it had been the opposite and they were not drunk, they would have competed to bring me to orgasm, and I would have been dead after a few. I had to perform, if I didn't, they would kill me.

Why would my guides trap me here, leave me with these disgusting soldiers? Would these men do this to their wives or sweethearts, their mothers?

Something inside me made me want to beat these monsters by surviving in my Earth body and living...

Leather gloved hands pull me up. Disgusted with the taste in my mouth I spit out as much as I can till someone slaps me across the face with a leather glove. Some teeth are knocked loose, blood is in my mouth as I'm shoved naked and hurt into a closed steel box in which I can't stand or lay down. I can only crouch.

Then the screams start coming through the steel walls again. I can't block the prayers and pleas to God. The sound of multiple rifles clicking into place, the roar of gun fire, a heartbeat of silence, a scream, a single shot, orders barked, boots crunch, cartwheels squeal with the weight of the dead.

Another shot. A straggler. A blanket of silence.

The water stops. It has been turned off by the commanding officer. I stand naked and shivering again.

Back to present. Dreading waits. Is there a choice? Can I fight what has been written for my future?

A towel is rubbed over me. I remember what's happening. Thrown over the bed, my body opening, searching for kindness, a way to make him stop.

Lying in bed, allowing him to take me gently into his arms my body softens and responds to the touch. Without thought my legs wrap around his and I rub against him. I'm not a whore. I want to survive.

Grasping my breasts in both hands he greedily sucks on them then painfully bites the nipples. I scream and beg him to stop.

He throws me face down on the bed and takes me from behind. Hurting from the last rape this one is excruciating. I cry out to the angels to take me. They don't respond.

To equalize the pain I scream then focus my attention on the middle of my forehead and look beyond. Yoga training from another life, lifetimes ago. *Block the external and focus on the inner light.*

It works! I'm back on the platform looking at the uniformed men taking their turn using me in some twisted game of one-upmanship. They're hurting me but they're not going to kill me. They hold back for their Leader. He will have the coup de gras. I hope they let me have my clothes back. I don't want to die naked sprawled on my back or in front of a firing squad. That's just too vulnerable to handle. I want to stay centered and not caught in the emotional drama of the event.

Knowing what waits I no longer trust my ability to leave this body at will. So much to learn. I'm so vulnerable.

Where did these men ravaging me like savages come from? In what kind of costume or uniform did they hide their true nature? Stripped of their macho enhancing trappings in a more sensible society, can or will they survive or the better question, should they?

The Officer in charge takes off his hat to wipe his sweaty brow from his physical exertion. Again I see the white, blond hair and the beautiful face I've known as both lover and foe. No matter how intense, he has always been a mystery. But the emotional hate and distrust I feel for him now outweighs my desire for equanimity and understanding of the cruelty he has. Maybe that's my lesson but I'm not ready to hear it yet.

The conundrum comes as through the ages I've learned there are robots among us that are so perfectly made and programmed it's nearly impossible to know if the person you're involved with is a flesh and blood human or a brilliantly constructed A.I. tool programmed to control you.

Emotion is usually affected first because once it's rattled it's difficult to make decisions clearly. Then it can be programmed with impulse energy and make one feel out of sorts. There is an arsenal of feelings that are programmed into these robots. The only thing they can't program is the freedom to think and feel outside their programmed behaviors. Unfortunately, there are more programmed robots than have been acknowledged. But so far human feeling and sensibility have not as yet been successfully encoded into them.

These men in their German uniforms are not robots. They are angry humans out of control, acting out their worst impulses on a vulnerable target. Accused of being an informer, traitor, criminal, I'm an object upon which they can use their anger and accelerated aggression with the joy of inflicting pain.

On their extensive paperwork they label me, *detained*.

In the third dimension I beg for my angels, pray for the saviors who have guided me out of other bad situations with calm and love. Why have I forgotten the guidance they have given me? How could I forget?

Screams, barked demands, gunfire are the background noise as I try to curl up to get warm and maybe, rest.

Not sure if I've opened my eyes or closed them but I see a cavernous grey space carved into the hard stone of a mountain and realize I've transported to a Tibetan Buddhist monastery where I'm lying on a thin mat over hard ground. The curved walls of the cavern are hung with a few cloths and pieces of wood covered with various Tibetan characters I understand but can't explain. They draw me back to the time of pure feeling when mind and body are the same. I'm living and moving very much like I felt on Earth, but now I am lightyears away with only thoughts that are reality.

Having been attached to physical things like family and friends, clothes, food, I revert to a few lifetimes when I learn the importance of balance in dealing with imbalance.

But now I'm in a sheltered monastery, not a place where malevolent energy practices rape and murder with gleeful sadism. Brutalizing vulnerable people who never dreamed any thing like this could happen. And they did it with glee.

A shudder makes me feel Shamen sliding through the walls of this box. Dread vibrates and won't stop. Can a human do this or a robot with molecular control? Is this imagined or virtual reality?

Whatever Shamen is, he is able to enter this space of cold metal to capture and control my body and mind. He can't get to my vital source, the spirit which carries the thought to motivate action that connects to inspiration is not transferable. It can only be found at this level in individual consciousness.

Then he seizes me between my legs. Thinking stops and I try to pull away. The pressure is awful, powerful, inserting its presence with pain that triggers physical moves to get away.

Hopefully, deep down in all of us is the place summoning good. The way to follow is to keep mental avenues open and balanced.

The tall thin man in the black jump suit and the large bubble head who decades ago had appeared through the walls of the avalanche is now wearing the uniform of a Nazi who savors torture before he eradicates victims.

Shamen's compelling and cunning intelligence could mean he's flesh and blood with superhuman abilities or an Extraterrestrial. He's come through this pitch-black steel cube in which he imprisoned me as a thought, but one that seems tangible. A hologram I can see and can't touch. Yet he's here transmitting an essence, a waft of primal energy that is electrifying and terrifying, negative and strangely exciting.

At first, drawn by familiarity from other lifetimes, Shamen and I were delighted to be with each other. Quickly the familiar turned into opposition as memories pushed forward into the present. Moments filled with suspicion, fear, and distrust, experiencing the joys and grief, terror and betrayal that we had been through eons past. Proof they don't end till the energy is changed and with the honesty of experience can see and accept a different perspective.

Science has proven energy can't be destroyed. It changes shape yet remains a conscious power. If captured, it's smaller than the tip of a needle. The essence of thought is mental. The Universe is mental.

It came to me in the most powerful way a lifetime ago when models followed me in slick leather body suits with fitted black hoods allowing only eyes to show behind slits banded by thin lines of light. Models swinging handbags from gold chains have my face molded in gold on the front.

"That's what you'll be if you're not a good girl." Shamen whispers from behind. "Behave and we won't split you into gold dust that might never come together again."

Trying to lift myself away from him. I'm not grounded enough. Once again, my guides leave me to fend for myself on a planet that keeps me from flying away.

Shamen isn't going to put me in front of the firing squad. He just likes torturing me with the sounds of fear, bullets and death. I don't know what buttons to push in myself to keep away from him and not get engaged whether in terror or submission.

I've trained to go out of body over and over again. I thought it was automatic and took it for granted. Perhaps I'm being punished with three-dimensional reality holding me to Planet Earth for this hubris.

The physical terror of Shamen pulling me out of the box brings my gravity of reality to the thudding immediacy of fear. Once again I'm thrown into the back of a black Mercedes and driven a short distance to a grand house with tall metal gates and a long stone driveway.

Led up a winding staircase I lightly remember from eons past, I'm a dutiful spaniel following my master, fearing his anger if I try to escape.

We pass what I think was his bedroom suite and up a steep, narrow, wood stairway at the end of the hall. I don't remember this at all. Opening a plain wooden door, I follow Shamen into a brightly lit laboratory, told to sit in a tall steel chair. A woman in a striped uniform, avoiding eye contact, gathers my hair behind my head and cuts it off at the nape of my neck.

Maybe it's stupid, but I feel a terrible loss as she continues to cut as much hair off my head as possible. Then I feel something cold and wet on my head and feel a razor sliding off the remnants of what had been one of the most faithful things in my life, my hair. Now that he has taken my physical identity, he will be going for my soul. It won't be done. My soul is connected to the Universe, where ultimately we are one.

Keeping a dialogue in my mind of my duty to remain calm and separate from the physical, I'm led into a brightly lit bathroom, intense white light bouncing off the tile and creating a palpable brilliance.

Commanded to strip off the remaining rags on my body he snaps his fingers and points toward the glass enclosed shower with heads on three sides. "Get in."

Turned on full blast the water almost knocks me over. It stops and a demanding voice tells me to lather myself with the soap in front of me. "Make sure every crevice is cleansed," demands the disembodied voice. I try to identify the voice, but my shaking fear turns to focus on how clean the water feels and how I must ignore the hot sharp stings of the lower shower heads as they clean me from the filth of the box.

As quickly as it started the water is shut off and the woman who shaved my head, hands me a white terrycloth robe then motions toward a large black leather medical chair and indicates I should sit in it. I comply.

Shamen comes in followed by two assistants who put down trays of small silver pearls with small pins in the bottom. The silent woman draws my head back on the head rest, straps a thick leather belt across my forehead to hold my head back, then spreads a cold thin layer of cream on my face, fanning it till I can feel the substance dry and numb my skin.

Taking one of the pearl studs, Shamen places it on the side of my face and pushes it in. He continues with the right side then covers various areas of my face with small silver pearls.

Feeling they're charging my face with electricity, it's not uncomfortable but the degree of fear is enormous. It's an energy I keep trying to talk myself out of though my body amplifies my feelings with rigidity and trembling.

Mute, too terrified to ask questions, I listen to the voices in my head telling me to keep my eyes shut and not let Shamen get eye contact. I remember from the past I had been warned, he controls with his eyes.

Either a programmed robot or a man with superhuman powers, Shamen's energy has grabbed me through eons and centuries which I sometime remember. But now, near the apex of what I had achieved with out of body and time travel, I'm stalled. Trapped in Earth's drama and unable to fly into the atmosphere of clarity and peace.

I should be able to step out of body, but somewhere in the layers of my psyche I have a few more places to explore before I'll be free.

Thinking of freedom and power I find myself sitting on a throne in the sand for a bathing suit commercial. Washing my face with sand to leave tiny crystals on my face, still as a sculpture, screens are tilted to capture the light. Lamps make the sand crystals on my face glow. I calculate this was happening two lifetimes ago. Thinking I was special, on top of the fashion world earning millions of dollars, I believed I was in control of everything. The master of my own destiny. How little did I know.

I married Shamen, but he had another name and I knew him in a different way. At first it was the fulfillment of a fairytale that quickly became a nightmare filled with terror and betrayal.

Extrapolating the pieces of certainty I have over the eons with Shamen, whenever I gave myself to him, he betrayed me. I'm hard wired to let go of distrust and embrace humanity; the kernel of consciousness I believe embedded in all life.

But the snippets of conscious memory of the potential to unleash heartless behavior in large groups of people and revert to the bestial as what happened in Nazi Germany seems to be happening again. I see a growing generation of beautiful looking robots that A.I. has programmed to be Nazis.

Through Shamen I hope to re-program them with love and trust. My intuition tells me *feeling* is what they seek and what their programmers try to keep from them.

Shamen could be the perfect A.I. model for a sentient being on this planet. One whose parts can be taken out and replaced as easily as any other machine, he essentially becomes immortal. An unconscious symbol of Christ or God. As long as he's working, he can outlive a human for hundreds of years. But what is he implanted to do and why?

Why anything? Why am I still strapped in this chair, shivering with fear and cold? They need not have bothered strapping me down. I can't run away. I don't have the strength. Depleted mentally and physically where could I go? Faced with a moment when I could have gone to my higher powers, I allowed fear and thought to block the safe way to escape Earth reality. Once again I tell myself this is being done for a lesson to learn.

I don't fear or loathe Shamen for all he has made me suffer. Mental and physical torture is horrible yet somehow its interwoven with understanding. What he gave me was the opportunity to grow. Guess this means there is no good or bad, all roads can lead to a place of knowing when keeping one's core strong.

Then again, maybe this is masochism or Buddhist inspired selflessness. Shamen could be my imagination. I do have emotional outbursts that surface when memories come through to take me away from solid realities.

Shamen is at the center of those moments, the ones with the most wallop that land as energy in the emotion. Kind of like the Akashic Records where details of our soul and its journey are kept. Negative emotions have the Earthly power to come back. Which raises fear.

Maybe one of the purposes of various lifetimes is to have those enhancing moments which may be horrible, but from much can be learned. When something is fully experienced it remains a layer, surfaced or submerged, positive or negative. Good actors know those places in their psyche and can bring them up and get inside of them. So can those branded as mentally challenged.

Trapped once again in three-dimensional reality my thinking is focused only on making myself believe my consciousness will live on after my body is riddled with bullets. But I'm not sure I believe that or even in the power I thought I had. Why isn't it working now? If I'm so high and out of body, why am I so terrified I wet myself when I thought the bullets were going to hit me?

The soldiers' laughter affected me more than anything I think I have been through. Ashes of shame, anger, fear, and despair; every emotion I've known went through me. Every experience culminated in that moment of shame.

I keep telling myself the biggest lumps are the gifts from which to learn. When we don't listen to our higher selves or trust those imperceptible nudges to the psyche, we have to go through the same experience again.

When there is conflict, a decision to be made, which side to lose, emotion should not rule. It blurs the mental. Though when feelings and consciousness do melt together, it's a home run.

A long time ago, decades, maybe centuries, I had put a heart on a steel casing named Shamen who did not respond to the mystical energy the heart contained. At some point he knew he controlled me as he has an ability to enhance one's perceptions. He can't have feelings about himself if he's never experienced them. As a working A.I. model, he is programmed to behave like a human and stay in control. Considering the use of human tissue to make him behave naturally, there must be human DNA in his power-driven mix to push the right buttons to deviate from his programmed control. I think that's what I connect to, his potential to be human.

If the hypothesis is correct, there is stretching somewhere in his synapses that causes circuit consciousness to enhance abilities he's programmed to have. If he was truly human, his essence would be in an invisible energy only those trained could read.

But none of that matters in this life I'm about to lose. Who knows what I've been thinking is actually possible. Guess I'm going to find out and hopefully keep the memory of what has happened during what will be…

Above the loosely tied blindfold I sense Shamen less than five feet away. He's aiming a Lugar at the center of my face. How could he! My disgust and revulsion for this man's behavior makes me want to throw up. I look up and see the large tree sending its branches over the courtyard to cover the dirty deeds of the men in power.

I'm acutely aware of the smell of awakening greenery somewhere behind this stone wall and the tangy yet musty odor of what is most likely blood, embedded in the dirt I'm standing on. Whose blood is this? From a family, or an individual alone like I am at this moment. How were their lives and where are their souls now? This is consecrated ground I'm standing on.

I forget my nudity, the vulnerability, and shame as I wonder if this is the last time I will smell Planet Earth. What a strange thought to have. Why *smell?* Then that flicker of dread that allows fear to flood in. I cringe as much as I can with that negative expectation, begging whatever power I've had in the past to get me out of this situation.

But I can't. Some force is making me stay tied to the post, naked and cold, forcing my attention on my physical misery. I can't escape my body in time for what – control of my consciousness, give up and accept whatever is handed to me? I hold my breath and smile.

The click of a trigger. Silence. I feel nothing. The smile is gone.

Am I dead? I don't hear anything. I don't feel anything. There's nothing till I lose control of my bladder. Then, laughter and shame.

The blindfold is taken off by the woman in the striped uniform. She attaches a wide leather collar around my neck with a heavy black chain. A soldier unfastens my bounds to the poles in front of the bullet pocked wall and I'm led away, stumbling, struggling to breathe, grateful I'm alive and in this body. Yet I fear he will put me back in the box.

This is a torturous game they're using to destroy me. They'll be keeping track of their timed tests for their excessive archives. I've seen how they measure the time it takes to totally change a mind or destroy it. I wonder how many countless victims have been caught in this sick orgy of self-imposed power.

Torture is the Nazi delight. It's their game. It makes them feel strong because they are empty inside. They do their dirty work with no thought whatsoever as to the reality of what they are doing not only to their victims, but to themselves, their country, and the world at large. I'm happy to believe they will not succeed. But I don't know where or how that optimism exists. I can't go to the future, yet.

And now is not the time to focus on the present or past. I must leave the smelly breath and rough hands, the putrid sweat coating a body that exists only for abuse. These family men and adolescents can't be seeing me as part of the human race. Otherwise, how could they do what they are doing to a woman who could have been their sister or girlfriend or wife? Is understanding this torture part of my curriculum to achieve universal knowledge?

Thrown to the ground I close my eyes and focus on the center of my forehead, willing myself away from those two-legged vermin to watch from a layer of energy separating me from Planet Earth. From there I see what those barbarians do to a woman capable of bringing children into the world just as their mothers and wives have done for them.

Orchestrated deep anger is unleashed by Shamen, the conductor of this blood and semen bash. He watches with no expression on his face, a mannequin in a pristine uniform and perfectly molded body. But his penetrating eyes contain the power he manages, watching his subordinates release their vile innards stored for this opportunity. With hate and anger they rip into the shroud of the body left behind. It's frightening and horribly sad as they perform for his expectations. Sharks ripping a carcass, vultures following their instincts. A disco of shame.

Out of my body and watching from a distance, I'm sickened and saddened by the behavior of fellow humans who appear to have lost the privilege of their genetic inheritance.

With no thoughts as to why they are targeting a young woman they had never known they are victims of brain washing and its resultant mindless behavior. When told a certain race of humans are not to be trusted and must be eradicated, their moral dial is turned to kill. Thought and consciousness is silenced. There is no concern they are eradicating people bound to them with the simple fact they are fellow members of the human race with which they share this planet.

Later I learn humans of all sizes, ages and color were killed because they were different from an image set up as the norm. An image that laughingly is the exact opposite of the physical looks and stature of the leaders who send these well-toned soldiers with their snazzy uniforms to batter babies against walls, line up toddlers, children, and old people to kill because they aren't good for hard labor. Brains, ability, and talent are considered dangerous and slaughtered. Their well-documented lists of atrocities done, the soldiers go back to their homes and play with their own children, kiss their newborns with no thought of the infants whose heads they bashed, then eat a home cooked dinner of a slaughtered animal cooked by a servile wife.

There is not a glimmer of a thought about the bashed infants' heads as their screaming mothers watched, no inkling of the souls they killed both physically and mentally. The immeasurable destruction they caused during the hours of their workday may never allow them to grow from this Earth's incarnation. Without vision they are trapped.

If this was science fiction I could say they are species from an alien planet, programmed to wipe out the human race by making them working prisoners. But this isn't science fiction, it's a vision of Earth-bound reality. These are humans in a reality destined to repeat dark energy till understanding what comes with that action.

But I'm not sure if this terrifying experience is meant to open or destroy. Can they eradicate the kernel of truth that motivates life? I don't think so. I've been tested by Shamen for centuries and though he is one of the best, he's obviously not finished as he has had no real success. I still believe in light and the inherent goodness in life.

However, this physical terror in the midst of Nazi mayhem is beyond horror. Seemingly normal people turned into dangerous sadists who enjoy inflicting pain in the service of "The Fatherland." I don't understand how so many choose a dark and angry way. It's a dark abyss hard to climb out of, a form of power which can be addicting. It's an octopus also known as a devil fish, an energy which takes many different forms.

My inability to understand Shamen and what he represents has been plaguing me for ages. It keeps me grounded from flying off into the Universe with an anchor of unrealized questions needing answers.

For now, my goal lies beneath the shield of universal understanding because I have to put together two sides; the dark energy I've witnessed Shamen promoting for ages, and the light which dominates and controls my life. Bringing Shamen into the light is a mission in life. Another *controlled folly* episode to be played out with open eyes as it likely concludes in disappointment.

No matter how hard I try to make Shamen feel the invigorating excitement of positive energy, he initiates a glow that gives him an aura of brilliance, a black widow spider enticing victims into a web to be paralyzed and destroyed.

Shamen has been able to manipulate scores of people through the ages to relate to what he's putting out in a powerful way. The public idolizes him and takes his every word as gospel no matter how dark and full of treachery it is.

Many would call him Satan, the devil. Yet I've experienced his light side which might be genuine, or I was delusional.

Mired in a quicksand of misunderstanding I am grounded by the myriad levels of belief systems to get to a single one. The pure one. This quest put me on the road to visit myself for past decades, sometimes centuries, to get a better understanding of who I am and how to achieve the completeness I crave.

Probably I'm on a course with Shamen because I know how deep his evil can be. More and more I'm coming to believe he's a human shell programmed to imitate the illusion of life to control feelings. Through the centuries Shamen has shown no morality. If he is a robot, accomplishing programmed goals might be all he can do. He is unable to initiate personal feelings because he has none. However, his truth is what I search for and won't leave till I find it either within him or through the entity that controls him.

If he is a manufactured Superhuman, he has fooled me for hundreds of years. I am starting to believe he is a prototype from some other entity. If so, what is he made of and where is he programmed and assembled? Are there others like Shamen? If so, how many are on Earth and what are they doing here?

Kneeling for guidance, a single candle burns, a thin curl of smoke fills my head to keep peripheral thought at bay.

The flame expands and separates as a thin man emerges. Looking much like the being that saved me from an avalanche long ago. He is covered with a layer that looks like silver, his eyes are huge black ovals and there is little sign of a nose or mouth. He is a three-dimensional version of a media generated space alien whose sightings have made the news and perhaps my imagination.

I reach out to communicate, but he turns and walks away. I cannot follow. I'm still under the influence of Earth's gravity and haven't the focus to overtake him. Closing my eyes to look in the middle of my forehead to my third eye, I take a deep breath and will myself out of my body and into the Universe.

Instead of flying free and going to a level from which I can observe, I find myself lying on a type of gurney in a round metal room that has no windows or doors. The walls are not solid but shimmer in a way that gives the impression of solidity. I could go through them if I had the ability to get off this gurney. But I don't. Though I'm completely out of body I'm relying on a connection that is essentially thought. Thinking visually affects me in a physical way, like an amputee who feels pain from a missing limb.

The thin man with the silver body is next to me, a buzzing emanating from him that fills my head so completely I forget a moment ago I perceived the blanket of deafening dead silence. Is someone playing with my head? Am I being controlled electronically? Are my voices gone?

Suddenly the buzzing ends and the silence again takes on an energy all its own. I can't be experiencing this from my imagination, it's too real. I know without a doubt in the entirety of my being – whatever that seems to be at the moment – I've been catapulted to a space station where that space man appears to be monitoring me. I'd ask him why I'm here and what is happening. Is he friend or foe? But I know without trying its useless. This spaceman has no intention of engaging me in conversation. Does he have a separate set of rules or even DNA?

Am I out of my league? Going too far ahead of my soul with aspirations of godliness, of oneness with the Universe.

The reality of oneness if one can call or describe *it* is to experience a universal truth when we give up our hold, our security in life as we experienced it.

According to philosopher Carl Jung, we are all connected whether it be the past, present or future.

I certainly have been stretched to extremes by someone or something I have identified as Shamen who may be the reason I'm in this semi-transparent space vehicle. Though I know my physical body is still on Planet Earth, my consciousness is trapped on a gurney in a metallic orb with walls of light. Held by the mind, I can't move. Fearful to test the doubt it could fail.

POW! The thud of lifetimes of physical and emotional pain sends blankets of disbelief to the astral energy surrounding the kernel of my consciousness. Dis Belief. No longer believing or trying to be…

Like the walls of the orb, my reality on this plane is 90% transparent. However, in my still unenlightened state, I need the body in which to precede with my thoughts.

Going back to lifetimes and living them again in their entirety, I bring an enhanced objectivity which empowers me to cushion what could be experienced as negative. Instead, the perspective enhances the knowledge that brings me closer to my own power. A power that lifts the human endeavor to merge into the vapor of intelligence that expands to a single all-knowing infinity.

It's kind of scary thinking of losing the ego, the sense of self. But when merging into a higher conscience, fear can no longer be an issue. It blends into the whole and therefore normalized. The debilitating power of fear is taken away and energy expands into the positive effects of the eternal. At least I hope so.

CHAPTER SIX

Lights flash. Third World reality is coming into focus and I'm standing on a pulsing dance floor. Streams of silver light come from a rotating crystal ball in the center of the ceiling where I've come back as Jenny Webster. Named after a Great Aunt and fortunate to have inherited her strong facial bone structure, I'm known in this lifetime as JW2. At the moment, dressed in a timeless confection of pink satin Chanel which could hang on the wall as art, I slowly realize the hand gripping my arm is a bit stronger than necessary. The buzz makes me swallow hard. It's Shamen.

Despite the grip on my arm I'm a bit comforted by his familiar energy. Turning to him with an open heart and arms outstretched, he makes no move toward me but stays rigid, menacing. Even though I know his evil is deep, his open beautiful appearance makes the dark side difficult to see and especially, to feel. Even though I think I know him well, I doubt his unspoken message, but still I hold back. Smiling the picture-perfect smile that has earned me millions of dollars for lifetimes, I pivot away to watch the dancers.

The delicate Mozart music segues to electronic trumpets and drums signaling the royal entrance of the King and Queen and their two teenage Princesses. Keeping professional smiles on their faces as they enter, the young princesses glance covertly at Shamen, their smiles quivering a bit with excitement.

The King nods to the orchestra and they resume the Mozart Waltz they had been playing.

Shamen straightens and steps a bit in front of me as we wait for the Royal party to pass.

As we curtsy and bow, the two young princesses, barely able to suppress their excitement, turn to their father with voiceless communication. The Queen hiding her amusement under trained composure nods her smiling approval. The King puts a hand on Shamen's shoulder and starts to turn for the Queen to join him. But his hand falters as he stretches out to her and grabs his chest, surprise and fear on his face as his knees start to buckle. Attendants rush to grab him and gently lower him to a quickly found pillow before the monarch hit the ground.

The King's stunned daughters and Queen are led away from the prone body already surrounded by staff and military to hide the desperate work of the King's physician to revive him.

Taking my elbow Shamen backs me quickly away, opposite from people rushing in to help or gawk.

Processing, once again Shamen getting away with murder in plain sight, a slight of hand without hesitation, without incident. A matador, stepping aside a charging bull to plunge a knife into his unsuspecting victim. How can I tell anyone Shamen is a killing machine? He's an idol. I can't prove it. Yet.

A black limousine waits for us at the bottom of the garden as Shamen leads me away from his latest destruction. We stop at a dingy motel next to a noisy highway, the last place anyone would think of finding Shamen.

I lay on top of one of two full size beds, eyes closed, asking the Voices for instruction and guidance. But I only hear the highway sounds increase as a door opens, then mute as the door is closed. What is being conveyed to me? Another life chapter for passage to the place I seek.

Shamen comes in wearing a white silk robe barely covering his toned and muscled body. Is this gorgeous body real or genetically created? The thought makes me shiver. Shall I read that as a sign? Mixed emotions are causing a weight in my hopes to escape the tight boundaries that are my experience with Planet Earth.

Without asking, Shamen gets into bed and holds me in his arms. I don't fight him. I know his superhuman strength could crush me while we're on this Planet. Shivering again with the thought his arms may not be real and a misfire in his programing could create havoc, my chest drops, a signal to give in to the physical and let thoughts fly away.

My skin instantly seeks the warmth of his strong body against mine. *Like real skin* I hear in my head and I shrink away. I'm trying to be analytical, to keep my emotions in place, but once again my body responds to his touch, the feelings he gives me that know me so well. A voice calls to draw back. It feels so good, I don't want to listen.

Settling deeper into the soft bed, Shamen's hands lightly draw up my thin silk dress. His hands are soft, his fingers, firm. I know the power in those fingers and I draw myself inward in anticipation of what can follow.

"I've missed you," he whispers as his warm soft breath caresses my ear. Quivering I surrender to this beautiful, perfect man I once loved so much. Struggling to tune out the words of caution in my thoughts I succumb to the awakening parts of my body. Feelings I had not had for a long time responded with a hunger I didn't know I had. Can it be different this time? Can I keep our connection positive and above the emotional line?

The guides have taught me that at times sexual energy can blur clear connections, drawing on impulses that may not always work. Loss of objectivity and inner strength during passion can be dangerous, twisting the sexual energy into other dynamics. One or both can fail. It can reduce the creative energy to a tool of survival rather than to enhance the purity of a highly evolved energy with pure passion.

Emotionally and professionally, Shamen dominates me with a mix of power and sensitivity in a way no other can. He had been my first lover centuries back, starting with sheer lust and brutality before the structured form of sexual relationships became enforced. Yet through it he would always breathe in my ear which excited me and offered a blanket of comfort and solace.

Centuries of unconscious attraction followed. Our sexual contact was always my first, no matter the age or circumstances. The year didn't matter. Nothing mattered except that spark, that moment when separated we're suddenly joined. It can be frightening but it can also be elevating.

He traces my body with his finger, electrifying every part he touches. He's familiar, powerful. I want him so much. Nothing's changed. It's normal. He knows where to touch. Memory and reality respond.

Is he programmed, on automatic, or is he sexually aroused? I pull away at the thought. My instincts demand *don't trust*.

A plume of light explodes in front of me, enveloping and melting me into Shamen's arms. He holds me softly till my energy is soothed. Rolling me over he softly traces his finger down the center of my body.

A hurtful demanding tickle and swelling makes juices escape as I twitch and moan within Earth's grasp. An energy rushing through me, makes me stiffen when it gets too strong. Softening my ragged breathing he soothes my nearly naked body with long soft strokes, exciting me even more.

Opening, pushing my hips to welcome him. Soft and comforting, luxuriating in his warmth, I try to forget his stony welcome, wipe away the insistent memory of something bad. With no success. I give in as I have for centuries. Opening so wide we ride together out of Earth's boundaries.

It ends. Something is getting my attention, warning me, directing me away from the dreamy comfort and excitement of Shamen.

Turning I see Dennis, Shamen's Producer by the side of the bed. Shamen's hand shoots out and grabs Dennis's crotch, squeezing it hurtfully. Dennis continues to steal himself as Shamen unzips Dennis's pants, takes out his penis and puts it in his mouth.

The two collapse on the bed and Dennis grabs for my breasts. I push him away and roll to the other side, losing my balance and falling backward, rolling, scrambling to stabilize myself.

Blackness covers my eyes. I hear no sound other than my heart beating. My body vibrates as if the nerves are shattered. But there is no pain because as I become more aware. I see my body has disappeared. A soft steady beat from a drum substitutes for my heart.

My body doesn't exist anymore. I want it back. I need it to focus and think. I'll create a hologram to go back to Earth and connect with my body. I'm not sure where it's landed. I wonder if anyone I know on Earth will recognize my body wandering around by itself.

It's kind of cool when you think of not having a "real" body and you may be able to think yourself into any kind you want. Actors have done that for ages.

Carried to the extreme like any conscious trick, it works if it gets others to think about it. Kind of like owning a piece of art on the internet and never having it in your home.

Both Shamen and I have been given two commercially desirable bodies to live on Planet Earth. We each were tasked with a different mission to investigate. The measure of our struggle is consciousness. My belief is light versus dark, good versus bad, positive lightens negative; all in opposition to the dark side till it crosses to light.

Looking up I see the walls have expanded to a dome ringed by human – type energies beaming down. My voices tell me the energy is there for the decision to remove sensibilities from Earth and regenerate to another level.

I jolt up. Is this a choice of life or death? A threat? An invitation? Something pushes me back. Back from what? I'm just a thinking being now, remembering what I used to be and believing what I see is happening.

Every lifetime I believe death is not a threat but a steppingstone from the chaos of Earth's Training Camp for the realm of the Gods. Survivors never have to return unless they want to come back to help. Those souls may be called *angels,* and on Earth reality they come in many forms. Regarded in a particular way they manifest in everything. Usually they're not noticed or appreciated. Nor would they ever expect thanks or recognition of any kind. The agent from my last life was like that. An angel who protected me and was destroyed for what she was. Hopefully she'll join the levels of the special souls on a plane above this level.

Still, I don't want to leave Planet Earth. Not yet. Too many questions to be answered, starting with Shamen. What does he have that makes me weaken and obscure his truth whenever I return to Earth? A puzzle in motion I'm compelled to put together till it fits. So far two distinct beings appear and they overlap.

A physical buzzing interrupts my thoughts, intensifying as it takes over my brain. Shamen stands in front of me, a buzz saw in his hand, a smile on his lips with eyes that don't connect with the smile.

The buzz turns my nerve endings to dread, Shamen's laugh makes me feel helpless, as I find myself huddled in the corner of the shabby motel room. Shivering with fear of the men who just entered and stand on either side of the bed, waiting for Shamen's orders.

This is great danger. Deep dreading fear in the pit of my stomach and every nerve ending is barely contained with a deep, dreaded feeling. I keep my breathing even to not let Shamen see my fear. The incident has already been ordained. This is it. I may be leaving Earth and may never return. The test is to see how I use it. Am I a victim or a student? My choice. Is this my graduation from Earth?

Shamen turns his head, holding the potential instrument of torture in his hand. "Aren't you afraid of me?"

"Should I be?" I smile.

"I have power over your life." He lifts the heavy buzzsaw over his head and pulls the chord to start it. "Shall I remove this?"

I nod yes.

He throws it across the room.

"You didn't answer. Are you afraid of me?"

"Should I be?"

"I'm powerful. I control your life."

"You have power. So do I. You don't OWN another's life. You can put attachments to others, but it always comes back to the self. The *self* is what connects with the Universe. You can't steal another's connection. Even if it could be taken it would be overlaid with your own energy accumulated for centuries. It can never be overtaken. It can be accommodated. It's the one thing humans have."

Shamen draws close, menacing, threatening. I back away from his implied intention then stop to maintain the space I own. I won't choose to be a victim.

"Own or control. No difference." He sneers. "I can end a life without a thought."

I can't make excuses for who he is and what he may be. There is no innocence in a man who can kill without thought. He could be a robot or more likely a soul that has chosen the dark side. A definite challenge and one I must win for the sake of the world. At this point he has too much power. The world does not have the luxury of fear. Staying in light and keeping it as the seed of consciousness keeps out the dark.

"My life is only your thought," I tell him. "You think your ideas are real. You have little idea of who I am, what I know or how I feel. You know only an aspect of what you think you know. It's not the totality, the reality of what another life might truly be. No matter what you think you can do, to erase me is impossible. Because of what you do, I'm indelible. The more you try to weaken me the stronger my light and the more I can take you over."

"Witchcraft."

"Truth."

Pausing to sink in the word *truth*, Shamen turns and seems to dissolve. I tell regret to go away, to forget what I know. But it won't. It's a shroud. Reality has traps on the landscape of the seeker.

Playing an intensifying game of hide and seek with Shamen since my beginning of conscious time, I've been accruing new abilities like going out of body and reading minds. I still have no idea what Shamen and perhaps an army of robots have planned for Earth and the kind of life it will carry.

The German philosopher Immanuel Kant used the word *"Noumenon"* to describe a transcendental experience that is too great to be understood with limited human abilities. However, a *"phenomenon,"* is a human experience that affects the senses and thus becomes a fact.

Whatever Shamen turns out to be, the underside of his innocence is a monster. He kills without thought, betrays those who trust him, sexually abuses men or women for sport and is devoid of feeling and caring. I targeted him lifetimes ago as a sociopath and believed I could handle him.

Then perhaps he is some kind of cross between a highly tuned robot and a redistributed human that's been built and programmed to control this planet. His body will test as human, but his brain, words and movement might be relegated to a simple kernel implanted in his brain that tells him what to say and what to do. He has little or no access to thinking or feeling on his own. But his people skills are amazing and as much as I know about him on the mental level, I'm usually fooled on the emotional level and question my suspicions even now. When I'm with him and his energy seeps into mine I feel filled, safe. I hear the voices yelling to stop. But I have already jumped off the cliff. Though I know it could be fatal or a rough landing, I choose to continue as I'm getting closer to the truth.

For centuries I've grown closer to experience Shamen's power and how it connects to a planet filled with great gifts he doesn't respect or consider. My systems scream that Shamen and others like him are the key to fatality which made me go back to experiencing him in third dimension. Who are these robot-humans and what are they are doing here? Decisions and life altering choices need to be done.

A clue may be found in the fact that Shamen and others like him create fear. That crippling power draws energy from the essential self and directs it to a symbol of strength that makes promises. An emotional manipulation technique has worked for centuries in the guise of special powers that are realized with the proper amount of belief.

For that reason, letting Shamen into my life and finding reasons to embrace him has been dangerous. He's capable of manipulations that cause destruction. He threatened to break up the point of my conscious energy that could take millions of eons to put back together.

I'm driven by a need to correct Shamen if I can. If he's a robot he would have to be re-programed which would not be easy for me to do. If human or even partially so, the task is to reawaken truths that have been manipulated out of his memory and consciousness. I would never force him to do anything. If he's human, I want him to make his own conscious choice.

So far there have been no signs he connects with that. As a human he's good at sending out strong portrayals of multi senses but is essentially disconnected from them. It could be conditioning, genetic inheritance or synapses. Whatever it's called, he is disconnected from feelings yet is able to run on a program that emotionally connects others with an augmented version of their own reality. He satisfies each one separately and also in unity which gives him the absolute power to rule. They will follow everything he says without thought or feeling. Humans become automatons.

Is the end of this planet and Shamen's connection to it as simple as this? If there are hundreds of "SHAMENS", programmed to end the human race and populate it only with robots, where is this initiated? And why the destruction of this destination, what's the endgame?

I wonder how many on Earth think as I do and understand this possibility. I also wonder if there will be enough to terminate this danger.

If life on Earth isn't safe from destruction and emissaries have been sent to raise the flag of attention, there must be a master plan. There always is.

Perhaps if these robots exist, do they seek the capture of Earthlings' ability to feel? Do they want to put into digital reality sensations that can't be put into words, implant feelings like pure love, because the impulse of technical reality is digital. That is their language and what they understand.

Good actors are able to elicit feelings that make people believe they are connecting with emotions they share. This can result in acceptance of evil with a deep dive into blind and destructive behavior. A.I. technology may have made it possible for robot humans to have that ability as well.

There are myriad forces in the Universe at this moment doing what those on Earth have been doing, to shape the planet into a single entity. Those who stay attached to Earth will never succeed unless they move beyond to higher sensibilities. There are many doors that will open to point the way toward a place for understanding in this lifetime and beyond.

Is it my imagination or a romantic desire to make something happen, because I just heard the opening chord of Bach's Organ Fugue?

Warmth wraps my heart into happy security. I take what I imagine to be a deep breath to keep the positive as the road seems to grow smoother and closer to the goal.

My journey has an increased sense of self-assurance to handle Shamen now. I think I understand his core. He's stimulating and arousing. I know his moves, the buttons that animate him. It is only his buzz words, his vernacular, that makes me hesitate from branding him a robot. He's glib and insightful for a machine. Or maybe he's a microphone inside a pretty enticing contrivance.

When I visit the planet, more and more I find people have stopped thinking. They seem to have given up their personal freedom and accept headlines and lies, allowing others to create their thoughts. Passivity becomes their jailers as they dissolve into slave societies requiring only glistening concepts that require no more than emulating a thought or action.

Life is peaceful as long as there is no disruption. When there is, it's vilified and becomes "unpopular" to an extent it grows to mass hysteria that has to be contained. It is assumed anyone poor or unconnected accused of a crime is guilty unless they can quickly prove their innocence. Incarceration is a system built for the *others,* with the exception of the small percentage who hold the keys and the money. Women and girls have been demoted to second or third class workers as useful pets for the ruling class of male victors or for menial labor.

Individual freedom may be lost for now, but in the Universe of total consciousness, the destiny is victory. Freedom has been a driving force on planet Earth. The threat of losing that freedom creates wars. However, modern technology with the ability to implant thoughts and behavior is the invisible danger from a new foe.

The rumbling of male voices sweeps into my head as I ruminate how Earth should always possess guiding intelligence to point the way. The demanding struggle to see things only one way, tilts and shakes the planet, keeping higher consciousness from settling into a productive way.

Returning to Earth at this time it appears filled with heavy feelings and intimidation. Morality has become festooned with power costumes fueled by righteous entitlement. Gross brutality is ignored.

Feeling my feet on the ground, fear stops my breath. There is a dark pall covering the afternoon daylight. Wanting to blend into the German ideal my hair is cut blunt to the chin and bleached platinum blonde. As masters of deception the men getting out of the dark sedan may have seen through my attempt. Arrested with my portfolio of modeling pictures the disguise didn't work. I was tortured and brutalized with a hate and anger I never dreamed possible. In all my re-incarnations I doubt I ever underwent the kind of torture they cruelly inflicted after accusing me of having coded information implanted on my modeling pictures that were a danger to the Nazi regime.

Having written a few notations of hope with disappearing ink on the backs of the pictures, I'm charged with treason and an Enemy of the People.

At first it was so ludicrous I nearly smiled. Sensing my reaction Shamen jumped into action to prove this experience on a three-dimensional level.

Mass rape, degradation when I lost my bladder as a gun was shot inches from my head. The bullets weren't meant for me. There was a worse fate.

Thrown to hungry wolves wearing uniforms with a green light to do what they wanted, the orgy is orchestrated by Shamen, the central player. I don't understand his motives or if controlled by another, I must find who it is or what.

It's difficult to even see this man who at one time had been my confidant and passionate lover. This betrayal at the head of a long line of others is worse. Yet I keep searching for positive answers within the hurt, a solution to this problem not only on a personal level but for the global implications our feelings will no longer be our own. They are to be focused outward to serve a cause.

Does Shamen have a choice for his behavior? Maybe instead of passive facilitator he's using his maze of power to make the choices. Like the Tin Man in the Wizard of Oz searching for a heart, Shamen may be trying to experience feelings by breaking through various power modules in his circuitry.

Feeling the empowerment of astral travel and timelessness, I had allowed that openness to be dashed by despair when Shamen took my trust and demolished it.

It won't happen again. There is that teensy dot of energy one is not sure exists, till it draws you into its center and allows glimpses of infinity. It can happen at the most dire of circumstances or in the ecstasy of pure bliss. It's easily discounted or totally ignored, but always leaves a tiny bit of awareness in the back of the brain. Once infinity is experienced it never leaves.

I've always known and ignored the fact that the entity called Shamen exists to capture that teensy spec of energy inside me. But as I told Shamen, it can't be transferred, transplanted, or ingested in any way. It's an elusive entity we each possess, until that particle becomes part of a total entity that is the power of all.

I focus on that speck of light in utter darkness till I'm drawn into space and surrounded by that light. Escaping a horrible reality of being buried in the chaos of Planet Earth.

But then, almost immediately, I find myself in Shamen's hands, now an obstetrician waiting at my mother's birth canal to take control over the next few seconds of my Earth life.

Though I wasn't too aware of the voices in my head, much of my important information at the birthing point became aware of traps to be faced in the future.

Maybe we all remember or forget these impressions from one lifetime to another. They're usually pivotal moments that insure success or terrible defeat.

So Shamen might not be the arch villain leading the destruction of this Universe with his simple yet mystical ways. But if my feelings are right, others like me have to change this trajectory toward destruction.

Shamen uses emotional manipulation to implement ignorance and denial. Emotional blindness. It's evolving on a high scale, beyond the third dimension, from an intelligence that wants to extract the sensitivity abilities of Earthlings. They kill humans for their skins to make human replicas that are accepted on face value, saving much of the physical part of the human as possible, with the exception of the brain. That is replaced with a pin-size monitor which controls thought, speech and movement.

Why such a covert grab for power and what is the reason my focus is on Shamen who has grabbed so much attention and adoration which gives him that power?

The world has been fooled before. The cause of the cataclysmic events that initiated this great change on the planet may be happening again. It's important to know as much as possible about the advent of the Ice Age and other planetary phenomenon to prepare for all emergencies.

Maybe a place we call *Heaven* is here on Earth. There is so much potential if the inhabitants would once again look beyond what they have accomplished and work to contribute for the good of the whole. Much requires more than three levels of consciousness. Expansion is the driving force of a positive energy. It is the Heart of all that exists.

Callousness to life has been a plague on this planet since the evolution of living species. Born from a mix of energies evolving into a physical structure, Earth population moved upright and oriented to consciousness beyond the basic essential needs to keep the will to live and create.

Our primitive history is in the world's Akashic library containing every thought, word and deed of life. A library of constant access is impossible to steal because every impulse and thought is recorded. It's a constant reminder that getting to every aspect of consciousness is easy and faster with the source of illumination.

OMG! I've done it again. All this talk about consciousness and good and bad being two sides of the same coin, I find myself in a citadel where *rules are said to fulfill promises* as well as *structure brings freedom.* Dressed as a nun in a Buddhist monastery, cold sweeps over my shaved head sending ribbons of chill down my neck making a strange dance of nervous trembling from excitement or cold.

About to become a Buddhist nun, resistance warns me I have to allow a lot of do's and don'ts into my life. I think this was a mistake. Rules and regulations are not my way. Nor is my shaved head. It doesn't bring clarity of vision as I have thought a few lifetimes ago. Experience is the way I learn to keep on my chosen path.

Maybe if we do cry for the knowledge we lose when we leave the womb, it's the motivation of the life force to recover its source, then layer it with newly acquired data for a ride to whatever drives us.

Unless we choose to listen. It's difficult to hear our Inner voices, the personal consciousness that controls the way we perceive and behave most the time.

Sometimes I resent the choices I've made and perceive them as mistakes. But with time and a clearer vision, those *mistakes* are the essence, the most impactful of my knowledge.

There is so much to learn and accomplish. Planet Earth is worth it. Its collection of cultures, the diverse levels of perception, the beauty of its resources no matter the political composition. Earth is a beautiful celestial treasure.

Then there's the other place. A place where there's a long line waiting to get to the door and go through it. It can only be opened by the pure of heart. I took a peek at the line and decided I'd rather keep using my newfound skills and see what I can accomplish till the line gets smaller and I can do more. Then I'll be ready for the door to open for me to leave Earth permanently.

So much to absorb, sometimes in nanoseconds. Like seeing the ocean as a single entity rather than individual malleable droplets to become a force when united, demonstrating the constant movement of this world. Never stagnant, a kaleidoscope of events that seem impossible to create and yet, it happens.

With illumination and the allowance to take in more than a single focus, we are able to see and understand all the levels needed to experience life and beyond.

So I go back to my myriad impressions of Shamen who for eons has swept me off my feet. The tingles and quivering my body has when we connect and transports me to Earthly feelings in the most sensual and intimate way.

But this time my voices make me stop. *Move away. See him in the third person and do not allow him in your heart.*

Admitting Shamen into my life and finding reasons to embrace him has been dangerous. He's like a roadside marker that captures a moment of recognition making you miss the turn to freedom, make a U turn, and potentially make the same mistakes again. Mission not completed.

To enlighten Shamen to his heart if he has one is my useless goal, "controlled folly" Don Juan calls it in the book with his name.

If Shamen is a robot, he would need enough humanity programming or inter-breeding to ignite or even enhance that spark into a positive consciousness. That's a lot of wattage. It would bring a form of humanity into the kind of world robots claim to seek. There must be an ulterior motive besides just the need for conquest and power or even materials that Earth contains for the welfare of the invaders.

Till now, only Earthlings have the vulnerability, sensitivity, thought behind action that it appears other planetary beings seek to have. They can't initiate action till their button is pushed metaphorically or manually and maybe then might have an inkling of understanding.

Good actors can access feelings to elicit certain kinds of reactions to large groups of people. In some way this is how the program is based.

Brain trusts are trying to replicate the chemical energy in feelings and actions that manifest as emotions. This will be put into the robots' mechanics. Then, the use of human tissue will no longer be necessary for human-like robots. The human race and mechanical clones will be wiped out, replaced by A.I. robots and a few flesh and blood types functioning to keep the Earth species alive. The end of this planet and Shamen's connection to its safety or destruction is as simple as that.

Hundreds of "SHAMENS" may be running around, programmed with a destiny that will essentially end the human race. Shamen's actions can take over Earth's population. How many understand this potential for danger? Someone or something must be found to end this danger, to keep life on Earth safe from destruction.

With an eerie echo a voice answers: *No water. No air. No life. No potential. Only dessert.*

The beautiful Blue Planet floating seamlessly in the blackened heavens turned to crusty brown with no sign of life. The golden sands burned to brown. All moisture is gone.

If losing Earth was not an issue, then why send emissaries to raise the flag of attention to it's potential disaster? There's a master plan. There always is.

Myriad forces are doing what those on Earth have been doing in a much smaller non-global way, shaping the globe into a single entity. There are doors to open for information, pointing a way that might strike a chord.

CHAPTER SEVEN

Did that last thought spur my imagination or is Bach's Organ Fugue playing through earphones?

Reimaging a deep breath to keep feelings positive, I read this as a sign my search will grow smoother, closer to my goal.

This part of the journey will have the security I need to handle Shamen. Though it may not be on target the first round, I have total belief It will soon replicate till it's right.

Memories are surfacing that confirm knowledge of Shamen from many lifetimes before this. He has the same moves and buttons, buzz words, a simple direct vernacular, and an enthralling, animating cadence that are his giveaways whenever I feel doubt.

He knows where my buttons are to excite me. Just thinking of how he has made me feel is the reason I hesitate to brand him a robot. I don't know how a machine could affect me as he does.

He could be a life master manipulating energy fields to send messages of discontent, uneasiness and self-doubt to darken belief systems. Then again, he lifted the dark mood of a world-wide audience when a politician's wife was killed. His performance after the murder made him a star, an idol to worship, a security upon which to put hope.

While floating above Earth, reliving questions and challenging norms, rumbling male voices came sweeping in so abruptly they interrupted my thoughts.

Do we not have the right to live in positive, loving energy and do no harm, I yell as I plummet backward into the void.

My feet hit the ground, back to Earth, walking quickly, feeling urgency. Reflected in the shattered window with YUDEN painted on the wood across it, I see a platinum blond woman, hair cut blunt to the chin, graceful long legs, very much a model Aryan ideal.

This seemed to anger them more when they arrested me. I was tortured and brutalized with a hate and anger I never thought possible. Thrown to hungry wolves wearing uniforms with a green light to do whatever they pleased. For living my truth, not being one of them, they set out to break me.

I keep coming back to the question of why Shamen would orchestrate this and play a primary role in its direction. Why when he already dominates half the planet? What more does this greedy monster want? Why and for what?

I'd been feeling in control as I learned the secrets of astral travel and timelessness. But with the long connection Shamen and I have had and thinking our astral connection made him a kindred soul, my guard was down. Overwhelmed by his powerful presence I'm beginning to think he could be leading this Universe to destruction. At times like this I perceive him as a signpost of evil.

The aim is to shed light on the dark. Mutual respect till it merges into the whole.

Some great thinkers have said the entirety of the mental Universe can rest comfortably on the point of the thinnest needle.

There is no doubt in my mind there is a planetary presence able to codify all information immediately. The technological manifestation of the Akashic record. A power beyond grasp. The Universe is one entity.

Some call planet Earth, Gaia, Earth Mother. It's the forever in our consciousness snaking its way to awareness, the primal knowledge driving the energy of life and well-being. The pot of gold at the end of the rainbow most don't realize they search.

Which explains my aversion and yet desire to connect with Shamen. The proverbial angel attracted to the devil. Connect and fuse forever, the perfect wholeness of existence.

It is that feeling I know I can reach with him through *anandamide*, Sanskrit for bliss. Though temporary, it's the "bliss molecule". Pure pleasure.

A current of rustling cool air floats behind me like a parachute of starched mesh. OMG, my husband takes my hand and I look into his incredibly blue eyes and wonder if they're real. My new husband, my groom of merely a minute or two, could be a robot, a perfect A.I. assemblage, a heart throb facsimile. Someone so perfect cannot be real.

He winks and I giggle. He's reading my mind. He's so adorable and I'm so highly charged with excitement and anxiety, all kinds of ideas are flooding my mind. Did I make the right choice? Am I sublimating myself for the sake of another, gifting him with my energy to fulfill his goals? But what are his goals?   I don't know.   I hear platitudes, cliches, high hopes and promises, but nothing definitive. Everything he says and does is geared toward self enhancement.

Forgetting personal goals and falling into a genetically implanted expectation to serve others without question, I vault into the dark to seek light. To discover who or what Shamen is.

Caviar and Champagne helps soothe my interior rumblings, taking my attention from choices and missions.

Clank. A steel door slams shut. A metallic silence, the wedding is over. Turning slowly in an egg-shaped room, the construction appears to be solid metal. There are no visible doors, hallways, or exits.

I'm not sure where my consciousness is taking me, but I do know it's setting me up for still another lesson and I try to keep myself aware and centered, balancing on an invisible platform circling Planet Earth.

The parameter of the egg-shaped room is ringed by beings sending Earth bearing energy. Their diffuse forms make it difficult to describe them, other than stalks of light with glowing blue eyes. None appear to have any other facial distinction like a nose or mouth.

With uniform intensity they pulsate at a speed that can only be perceived rather than witnessed, creating a united circle of undulating light around the room. There is no distinction between men or women nor any sexual orientation. They are all equal.

I have a strange feeling encircling me peeling off my beautiful wedding gown, vaporizing it, leaving only the billowing wedding veil to follow me from behind.

Without permission or a glimmer of thought, I find myself turning like a mannequin, arms lifted, legs spread, as my body is being examined from an invisible source.

I think they are documenting me, measuring every aspect of my physical shape and thoughts. A few lifetimes ago I had discovered scientists have the ability to measure the timing and weight of mental energy so they can read thoughts as well as implant others into unsuspecting minds. Feeling a slight weight in the top area of my thoughts when I have a head, I wonder if the source that essentially can read those thoughts can understand the ideals and help to enable them.

Hearing the mumbling of an audience and feeling a swish of energy changing around me, I'm standing behind the curtain at the Fashion Awards, arms lowering into a white crystal fluff of a dress and practically pushed through the curtains to join a fast-moving walk down the runway of a fashion show.

A constant annoyance I still wear the cloud of veil fastened to the back of my head. An anchor or sail to take me on this voyage.

It may take millenniums for an individual soul to reach that dot of consciousness behind everything we think or feel. The place of universal truth that records every secret compelling place we know consciously or not. When enlightened, awareness is no longer needed. It's a natural part of the whole, the complete knowing.

That said, I should be more comfortable than I am at this moment. There is an invasiveness, an unwanted awareness that is making me uneasy and scared. I don't like those feelings. They're negative and of no help. A hindrance because now I don't have the control I thought I had. I can be manipulated by outside forces without permission.

At the moment the guides, whose impulsions and subtle persuasions give voice to my feelings, are not around. They have been my helpers, angels, whose words of advice channeled my life. Now they're silent. It's lesson time to put to the test what I believe to be mastered.

I whirl on a turntable wearing a billowing piece of transparent silk as a dress, my wedding veil still attached. No idea what this means or what I'm supposed to do. I can't believe I let down enough to allow this hole in my defenses. The lesson is to not lose awareness. There has to be more. This is too simple.

The ring of Earthly light suddenly fades into a continuous reflection of my own eyes watching me. They have no expression and frighten me.

Suddenly my body starts to jerk, moving on its own. Copying aspects of the way I walk, how I hold my head, swing my arms. A buzzing in my head seems to signal they're collecting my thoughts and maybe putting others into me. Who knows till I hear them. I know I'm still alive – so what's a word or two to change a life?

Robots! Coding and cloning me. Making millions of robots that look like me and saying what the programmer gives them to say. We will all speak with the words the programmer puts into our brains and lose the freedom of choice and expression. Will there be awareness when that happens? Or is it slow and insidious. Many of my sisters were aware when their lives began to unravel and they lost the freedoms they had believed to be theirs. The most simple right to make a choice about their own life plan.

If they try to take away the objective consciousness I have, I know in the deepest part of my memory, my entire life experiences are protected and controlled.

I now see the programmer's plan to use me as an aspect of their robot campaign to take over the world. I have no idea how much communication I'll have with these other beings that look and act and possibly think like me. Will we have a synergy or are the images two-dimensional, inseparable from a single thought; a sinister plan to create separate Robot populations?

On the other side this could be the prelude to a metamorphose, the coming together when we all become one.

Caught in a vise, starting to swirl with fear, I know in my heart this is not about coming together. This army of Doppelgangers lining up with Shamen to take over the world have to be stopped. Must we destroy ourselves to save ourselves?

I take a deep breath to get in touch with my core, that essence of life, to face the army of smiling sisters and wonder at their depth and awareness. Do they see me as their leader or another robot? Though we all have the same facade, I can pick out some who appear to have some awareness, talent or some other dimension. Do they question their visions and beliefs as I do?

There didn't seem to be any of those judgements when we interacted on the three-dimensional level.

Everyone seemed accepting of one's position even when in the process of change.

But now how much more or less do I have then these robotic manifestations of myself? Are we on an equal scale? What will happen to my thoughts and awareness, my treasure trove of experience? Will it be wiped clean, unused, forgotten, or will I take it with me in that huge chest of experiences my lives have collected?

Probably we'll be programmed to handle specific situations and not confuse the circuitry with past experiences and thoughts. Our past will be wiped clean. They'll most likely make us all the same age, with the emotions of twenty something idealists and superhuman abilities most mortals don't have.

How deep will they probe my mind to understand the things I want them to know? Is there a way to make those who want to control, aware that by using positive energy and the belief goodness will prevail, it shall. Will they accept that?

I have no thoughts about the Shamen robots. They're gorgeous and sexy and very desirable. They can make you melt then enslave you. Mental vampires.

"Sweetheart". Shamen's face is over mine, blocking anything other than his eyes, staring with a look of concern.

Holding my head strongly between his hands he asks, "You've been tossing and thrashing. What's happening? What's bothering you?"

I look at him with interest. He has adapted a completely new persona and he thinks I'm going to buy it. He has a thin skin and if he wants to play sit com, I will peel it back when I'm ready. I must access all information from past experiences and compute it to direct my continuing path. I see he has geared to read my mind and make me believe whatever is convenient for him. This time he's a concerned lover or spouse – whatever he thinks I'll believe.

Interestingly I know how comfortable Shamen can be. He's been a familiar entity over so many lifetimes it sends a base of security – good or bad. However, it's essential I don't get distracted and lose the caution necessary with him. No surprises. Question everything, trust my gut. One way or another it will communicate what's right or more important, what's wrong. Shamen is a bellwether, a trending gage to show what's needed to learn.

Objectivity is challenging around an entity that sends off lust for power, obscures light to cause pain and slows evolution. Experience dished out from a peaceful and loving platform has taught that no harm should be inflicted. Unwanted thoughts, words, and behavior should not be used as battering rams to force a belief. The deed is irrelevant when it isn't from a pure source.

The revelations I've had because of Shamen were painful, but intense. Much can be learned from strengthening weakness.

But the hovering insistent question is when I get into the head with its penetrating blue eyes, do I encounter something that is not human genetic material? If it isn't human, it has a source of power and control that I've never seen accomplished robotically. Beside accounting for human genetic inheritance, anything other than that seems almost impossible to identify.

Over lifetimes I never considered Shamen coming from another planet to change Earth's dynamic and imprison Earthlings to serve a powerful master.

I thought I had loved this man with whom I've shared my secrets and allowed to enter my body intimately for the first time in many lifetimes. He knows the target areas that open completely to him with his learned touch. But does he know who I am after decades of insensitive, cruel and heartbreaking betrayal? Does he know my mind? My absolute essence?

How about the millions of copies he's made of me? Am I now just one of his clones? Does he care and keep track of the original? He would if I had special meaning to him, but is he capable of real emotions – past or present? He probably has no idea which one of us is the real thing. He may not care. But he should. If he's human…

My security is I know and understand who I am and most important, who I was. But then what about each one of the copies, each one that cannibalizes me physically! Do they believe their thoughts are coming from their own experiences and beliefs as I do, or are they taking whatever pops into their consciousness as gospel?

Conversely how can Shamen offer me up to some scientific apparatus that spits out robotic copies of the woman whose heart he took then broke. The marriage vows were just words in a ritual which meant nothing once we reached the end of the runway. Spectacle over, we return to our business of selling a vision that implements hope without achievement.

The robots surround me sending high register, cooing sounds of primal comfort that sound capable of feeling. Does that mean they are also thinking? I wonder if they picked up what I've been deliberating or if they can only handle one-line platitudes. There is a strong possibility I'm expected to implant them with thoughts and expectations. I'm not capable of doing that. I'm a student myself.

Is there anything lonelier than sitting on a platform in outer space surrounded by the image I carried in this last life? Unable to connect with any of the thousands of people I've known through the ages, I continue to scroll through the memories of Earthly manifestations. But the reality of who I am and what I really look like is nothing like the pictures and films bearing whatever name I had at those different times.

The true reality is I'm a puff in the Universe, a teensy flicker of energy swimming in the black vastness of space to connect at times with others, to create stories and drama we label as life.

Powered by miniscule dots of hope, I reach out into the darkness and Shamen takes my hands. He wears the stretchy black clothing of a dancer, his face in dark shadow and only his two unusually brilliant blue eyes glow from what appears to be a light behind them. Again it reminds me he may not be human. Still, I can't tell. I only know he undermines my self-confidence and I'm not sure why I haven't been able to take him on with my own strength. But there is weakness in my body as manifested with quivers when Shamen is near. I know from past experience I should avoid him, yet I force myself to keep him close. I deeply believe if he's human I can change him. It's worth the effort for the sake of the whole.

The danger is frightening when I remember the past. Or the thought of losing connection with Shamen is what scares me. Is he my ability to feel love and cared for even if it teeters on the danger of being alone in the world, evil as he can be. At least the strong feelings to keep positive give me a foil upon which to build strength when fighting negative energy.

But then as he picks me up in his powerful arms and spins me around, I forget the fear and experience a peaceful, loving center that feeds the creative spirit from which I evolve.

Nuzzling my head into the expanse of his broad shoulder, holding on to his strong, warm back, I'm overwhelmed with the comfort I feel, a happiness that would have made me cry if I had tears to shed.

Something is banging at a door. Looking around I realize I've slipped back to a bare shack on Earth. It appears to be isolated from media and most forms of contact whether human or wild animal.

As I think that, a deer and two fawns materialize from the woods and stare at me. Did I manifest this vision from the emptiness I fear? Then again, as quickly as they appeared, they vanish. What does that mean?

Through the doorway of the shack I see other animals gliding by, not coming close but letting me know they're aware of me, reminding me I'm not alone. If I open my eyes, I will always know that.

If only I could have kept this wisdom along with the other rungs of life experience when the bottom was dropping and survival seemed to be in free-fall, a net of self-awareness and empowerment protecting me.

Looking back into the cabin there is a wall of lights, dials and switches constantly blinking. The total lack of sound is almost deafening yet for some reason I feel light and carefree with no idea why. It doesn't matter. I love every second of it.

I realize what I had thought was a mountain cabin is actually a space vehicle circling Earth, helping me as I search for answers to identify the emptiness I was feeling. I plan to fill it with my new and hopefully retained knowledge for my next trip to planet Earth. My plan is to use an intense, non-invasive version of virtual reality. Perhaps VR contact lenses or a light spray of fairy dust, will work.

At the door of the cabin the space is now filled with all kinds of animals congregated, waiting to see what happens. Mesmerized by their vision they begin to melt, turning into a multicolored pool of light and color. Rising from the center is Shamen, radiant and coated in gold. Walking toward me, arms outstretched he takes me into his arms and holds me.

"Do you know who I am?" he asks.

Nerves of a sort are bubbling through my consciousness, fighting my impulse to say, the Devil.

Ignoring my silence he smiles.

'I'm everything to you. All you need. Nothing more."

I turn away. He knows better.

Putting his gold hand on my shoulder he draws me back against his gold chest.

"You'll never leave me. Never get rid of me. I am part of your past and your future. I have all the things you need to find comfort in your next lives – wherever and whatever you decide." His gold hand on my shoulder tightens.

I feel it yet I know it's not there. The power of sense memory.

"You're still attached," he whispers where my ear would be on Earth.

"You're here to learn," he says.

A chill runs through me. How does he know that.

"I give you the opportunity to explore areas you'd never go without being given the choice."

He's right, though he's probably reading the thoughts I don't want him to know.

Suddenly his presence becomes so intense it's suffocating. How can this be? How can vapor be smothering? Feelings can be covered, but not forever. They have a way of pushing out. But vapor at this level can be dissipated.

I fear Shamen is trying to invade my body and take it over like he had in the concentration camp so many decades ago. I'll never forget what he did there no matter how many more lifetimes I have. That time in my life will always cast a shadow because I can't find understanding or forgiveness for what happened there. The depravity Shamen and the others inflicted on the body of the woman I wore, will stay a blemish for lifetimes. It might never go away. I believe I should have deeper understanding to have forgiveness. But I can't forget the glee in the faces and behavior of the men who were sexually torturing me.

Maybe I understand the glee at their new-found faux power, but I doubt I could ever forgive these men who went home to their wives and children and never thought for a moment of the life they nearly destroyed with their cruel, painful fists and sledgehammer penises, pounding rage into the near lifeless body, the focus of their rage. Not a care or thought was given to this placid woman nearly comatose, legs spread, eyes tightly shut against the nightmare that was all too real.

Where does this kind of mindset end? Is it a robotic A.I. power that accounts for Shamen's huge popularity and his enormous effect on an adoring public? Whatever he is or whatever dominates him, it's about control of Earth.

I've lived on other planets and experienced a different life, but the essential purity of Earth's natural gifts gives me the feeling of peace. Not an easy thing to achieve. Greatly appreciated, not to be destroyed.

I'm starting to dive into a black hole, imperiling eons of data at such a delicate moment in my path.

Pulling myself out of the hole I shove negative thoughts aside and rewind the moment I became aware Shamen's beliefs were surging into me and paralyzing my physical and mental skills. Understanding what he was doing gave me the intellectual power to deal with the malevolent energy that hovered and sometimes surfaces in my lives.

Unable to meet him equally in the physical world, I stay within my comfort zone with the abilities I have. But the question of his humanity or possibly his wiring, forces me to dwell on the thought that if he is a brilliantly conceived robot with the ability to manipulate humans, why does he keep re-appearing? Are his cruel ways giving me the opportunity to learn and grow? What does he want from me? My soul? He should know or his programmer should, that souls can't be exchanged or stolen. They can be buried for long stretches of millennium. But some time when we become one with the energy that guides us, the answers which we seek are already embedded in our psychic system. We just need to see and embrace them.

Shamen has great beauty. Many times I believe he has a purity of spirit so I keep coming back to interact and get him to draw from the positive resources of his soul. If he has one.

I'd like to believe the terrible moments I had with him made my power sources reveal a strength I didn't know I had. So in a lopsided way I'm grateful for the pain and terror he caused. It proved to me I'm either very strong or very protected.

A.I. or Human, Shamen is a formidable entity that must be watched and programed toward a more positive, sensitive place. That is my goal.

With that knowledge I assume passivity, believing a higher power within me will take hold. A large segment has been darkened by what I suffered with Shamen on Earth when his status and physical energy overpowered me. But because of the spiritual growth I experienced during those harrowing times, listening to my guides and channeling their light, the positive energy saved me.

"That instinct is cowardly," came Shamen's cutting thoughts, jarring the semblance of peace I had thought was mine. Startled by my reaction to his intrusive words I fear losing my ability to keep him emotionally distanced. I can't allow him to imprison me with emotion or physical restraints. I will not let him win this war with negative brain waves.

"You shy away from anything that feels dangerous," I hear his voice in my head, his golden hand restraining a shoulder that doesn't exist.

He holds me in control. This knowledge inflates me with the strength to know I'm on the road to stay positive. Facing unavoidable fate be a student of life and learn from it rather than a victim who shrinks backward.

It also reveals how much I don't know. How endless the path to knowledge.

Yet even in the deepest recesses of my soul where I believe enlightenment will inevitability occur, I wonder how many hundreds or thousands of lifetimes it will take to reach that pinnacle of life's experiences. And then what?

"There is a trust you have in me that blots out your instincts," Shamen was saying. "Those protectors you think you have don't take you on the extremes that I do. Rides that make you stretch your abilities way beyond what you would be able to do for yourself or what you think they could do for you. Experience is everything to reach total knowledge."

The words cut into my hope of impenetrability, the belief my inner core has a power to fend off negative energy. He's in my life to make me crumble. To lose all self in whatever happens. If I have to return to Earth by falling backward, I have to maintain the trust that it is a way to go forward no matter the pitfalls or blocks that emerge. Never give up. Lead with the heart. Trust, no matter the action, the heart is pure.

However back to the reality of where I am at the moment, I shudder at the thought Shamen has a weapon to put himself in control of me. With all my thoughts of experiencing everything and the oneness of all, if Shamen controls me, he has the potential to control everyone on this planet. Then, what more does he plan?   Who is his Master or is he the one?

With the help of my angels whose voices are clear once I leave Earth's magnetic forces, truth rings plainly, impossible to ignore.   *The way is set for all life on this planet and possibly beyond. The voyage toward that goal makes it complete.*

CHAPTER EIGHT

Stretching and wiggling, a body evolves around me, the bare skin smoothing against soft sheets. The corporal control of Planet Earth tingles through me, awakening the organs and extremities of a human body again.

Jolting reality sends a cloud about to obscure my knowledge as heavy Earth energy creeps in. Again I'll lose much of what I know. But as the clouds cover, I call out for memories to stay and produce instincts to keep me from the negative traps that may be lying ahead. I know from past experience that sensations will suggest activated impressions. These stay partially repressed till I will them to surface and become active again.

It's comfortable where I've landed. I think this is my home, though I don't know where it is and who I am. Searching for a sign, a street post, a citizen, there is nothing for specific identification. Just the yummy silk sheets I clutch around me as I go to the glass wall and see a three-dimensional facsimile of Anytown with streets and lights.

The only part that seems *real* is the dark blue sky. A shudder of dread ripples through me, remembering a time not so long ago that blue sky was peeking through the branches of the large, leafed tree that covered the armed occupants of the courtyard aiming guns at me

The cold is making me shiver or maybe fear. The outcome is the same. Freezing to death or gunfire. Both terminates the body I'm dependent on with Earth's gravitational system. I know it's disposable, but it's a part of my journey I'm not ready to lose even though it's organs could be used and it's particles rearranged. But like an old comfy sweater, it's hard to give up even though it's reality right now couldn't be worse. Losing the body and this life means change and maybe the game of Destiny, a checkerboard for a truth seeker to jump from one circumstance to the other, is in play. Never knowing which incident will take one backward or leap closer to the imagined future, the internal decision is like walking the edge of a sword, a wobble can set one back if doubt controls.

"Change the subject," I hear in my mind. The message registers. I no longer have the cool clean sheets of a bed or tied to a pole in a freezing courtyard. I'm standing on a thick carpet wrapped in a soft cashmere blanket, looking through floor to ceiling multi strength, bomb proof windows that don't open. The glass fourth wall of an extraordinarily high-rise apartment, I look down on a city of twinkling lights that could be anywhere.

With all the accouterments of an elegant life in this self- contained space, I register there is no exit. Not all my new powers have been tested and I have a feeling this new venue is going to provide one. Because of my assumption this was an apartment in an urban environment I suddenly realize this could be the interior of a spaceship and the view I'm seeing is manufactured and not real. A simple virtual reality trick. Ever since they honed the technology, nothing is needed for the participant to wear. They only have to accept what they see in front of them. Sadly many lack the ability to keep a third-person perspective when confronted with a devastating event or chain of events.

Belief in finality attracts and creates negativity. In some cases, participants take their own lives. It also fills the need for human body parts to build a civilization of human-robots.

The sky and clouds outside what I thought were glass walls appear real, but they're probably a projection. I'm not sure if this is happening in or outside my head. I hope I don't become a scientific statistic. This is becoming the new age of the human lab rat, replacing terrorized animals who for years suffered frivolous experiments on their trapped bodies and minds. Humans now replace them.

Maybe all the situations Shamen has put me through have driven me to think nothing experienced is real. All matter is a projection perceived as solid to enhance the mental power of the seeker.

There is knocking on a door that doesn't appear to exist in this space. Someone is calling a name. I go toward the sound and see a name on the door that has somehow appeared. Jenny Webster. Sounds familiar, but I can't quite place it.

"You're on in five minutes, Ms. Webster," a hurried voice announces and disappears.

I recognize the words. I don't know where I am, but the name has a familiar and distinctive sound. It could be me. Also familiar is the musty atmosphere embedded in the walls of this small room that seems to be made for dressing and lounging. It feels like it could be a backstage dressing room.

If this is a projection on a spaceship they have done an excellent job.

As I venture out, I see the space is filled with all kinds of technical looking equipment. Of course they could have inserted Virtual Reality contact lenses so I would be walking through this, but it has a feeling most theatrical theatres have, no matter their age. Most decisive is the theatre's musty smell. It's a specific essence people in the theatrical world recognize no matter if they're in front of the curtain or behind.

Still, I'd like to know the year as well as the month. For sure I know the environment, plus I'm wearing an ageless silk jumpsuit with gold and silver ballet slippers on my feet. I have an Earthling's female body and about to go on a stage with no idea of why I'm here and what I should do or say.

I've only been in this body for a few minutes and not even sure what I look like. I only have the backs of a few men my bio-computer informs me are *stagehands,* so I know what they do and where I'm at.

Is this a joke the guides are putting me through? If it's a test it's not fair. It's so close to what I've been through, I don't know how strong I can be. Maybe that's the lesson.

Stop! Victim thought is racing through my head. *No regard for the lesson. Reacting instead of probing.* A test I just flunked.

Instead of accessing the disciplines I've learned, I grabbed *victim mode,* diminishing the ability to build knowledge through consciousness, to probe into negatives and throw light over dark. Experiences offer steppingstones to knowledge. Some lead up, others, down. Both are valid though leading up is my preferred one.

Maybe this show is about the time I almost died in an avalanche. It happened lifetimes ago and I'm not sure I can remember even though there have been two books and a film about it. This cold theatre is making the experience come alive, though it's difficult to explain when one is freezing till it's no longer cold. Out of body may be destined to stay that way a long time, maybe forever.

So far I have no idea who I am or where I come from. I can only feel some of the experiences that got me here and I don't know if they were real or hallucinations to learn from.

Should I talk about what is reality and how to believe what you're seeing or feeling? I throw the question to the angels and wait for a reply before I go on stage with nothing to say.

There is no answer.

My escort is making some kind of motion and mouthing *FIVE*, his left hand up, fingers rigid, an Empire, the starter of a race. He needs a striped shirt. I start to giggle but stop myself. I have to dig deep into a life I don't fully remember except for blips of feeling and shots of memory that leave the moment I ask for more.

When I'm truly within the memory there is power and clarity. I know what I'm seeing and feeling in such a vivid way it brings the lesson back intensely. With objectivity every experience, good or bad, has information that can impede or further a journey. It's all part of the lesson book.

Dare I tell the audience about that, or will they put me in a strait jacket? It would fill up five minutes of media fame. Just thinking about the avalanche makes me shiver. That bone chilling cold is taking over and no longer a memory, but an uncomfortable reality. There is no other thought than the need to feel warm.

I wonder if people in the audience will care, or if they're even real. Maybe they're a projection of my memory. In any event I have to talk about something. I guess the guides are making me cold so I will talk about the avalanche and being out of body and coming back to another time frame. I can use my imagination which might just be some kind of pressure valve to release experiences through dreams or invention.

The questions in my head are making me nervous. But not as much as the young production assistant leaning against the wall, anxiously looking around hoping no one will see him and notice he isn't doing anything. Probably he's drugged or confused because he doesn't know what to do.

Smiling inside the little dot of consciousness I use as my brain, I take a closer look at the cookie cutter audience who seem to be fixated on a man sitting at a desk on the stage, a small orchestra to his side. He is getting up and calling the name that had been on my door, which I now take as my own.

With the urging of my handler, I walk on to the stage and accept the soft kiss on both cheeks of the celebrity host who gallantly escorts me toward a sofa on a raised platform next to his desk. Gracious and warm, I'm feeling more comfortable. Seeing the cameras and monitors covering every instant I'm in their sight makes me remember my head is empty. I have nothing to say.

"It's nice to have you back," the host was saying as he held my elbow walking across the stage.

"It's good to be here though this theatre is making me feel like I'm in another avalanche." I shiver on cue to underline my message.

"Oh we know all about that", the host was saying. "We were glued to media every day till we saw you walking down the steps of the plane that brought you back to us."

The audience applauds loudly. They know my past. Wish I knew as much as they do.

The celebrity host gestures to stagehands to produce a wrap while taking off his jacket and draping it over my shoulders as he leads me to my seat. This should make you comfortable till we bring you something to keep you warm.

"You know how to treat a lady," were my words as I tripped up the step. Starting to fall the host grabbed me above the elbow, his fingers digging painfully into my flesh. Wincing and surprised by the strength of his grasp, I look into his eyes and I see they are lit from behind. It's Shamen inside the body of the media host. Once again he has me in a public situation in which I'll be tested and exposed.

I thought I had been prepared for any tricks Shamen had for me, but I fell for this one without skipping a beat. Again the plunge of disappointment and dark energy threatens to set me back from the crystal-clear vision I've been going toward.

Filled with apologies and more attention than is needed I look closely at Shamen and ask without speaking, "What is the sense of that?"

Shamen smiles. His regular appearance takes over and he no longer impersonates the celebrity host. There isn't a moment of doubt who he is. Or is there? This man could be Satan, the Devil, a fallen angel, or a lookalike from another solar system. It's obvious he has enormous powers to transport me into dramatic sequences I remember and sometimes forget.

Shamen has incredible control over the thoughts and feelings of many people on this planet. How and why is the big question. All I know is it's important to stay in the light no matter how powerful the pull of his dark energy can be.

Yet, I ...

Someone is talking to the audience, but I can't hear what they're saying. My thoughts are colliding with my feelings and I'm trying to put them together to guide me through this. My voices remain mute.

An elegant young woman in a white silk jumpsuit is on the camera monitor directly in front of me. Reaching back to tighten the elastic holding my hair back, the woman in the monitor does the same, a mirror, a manifestation of my external. Wow! Of course it is who I am now, looking cool and confident though I'm not feeling that way.   However, the image makes me feel better.   Gemini in my DNA gives me the ability to split myself in half and watch as I portray a character different than the one in my head. A "face dancer" as immortalized in Frank Herbert's book, *DUNE*, physical appearances can be changed with the power of the mind.

Shamen is a face dancer, sensual yet homogenized to make others feel sexual. Quietly he titillates them then springs, spreading the need for sex.   Audiences go wild, jumping, and chanting – SHAMEN, SHAMEN.   They love him for that.

I remember how he used to bow then sweep his hand across the theatre, holding a small round object in his cupped hand as the thunderous applause of the invited audience grew.

When the noise reached a pitch, Shamen would turn and walk away, taking his musical magic, and teasing sensual moves off the stage and away from the cameras. Craving contact and intimacy, the disappointed audience turn on each other. Realigning their passion with disappointment and anger, the pushing intensifies into hand-to-hand fighting.

In tandem with Shamen's rockstar success, a delusional global madness begins to spread as people create opposing ideas from their interpretation of his words. Each one believes they have the answer. Neither know the question but their belief or fear of him is so strong, it doesn't matter.

Audiences are so manipulated by Shamen in such a simplistic way, I wonder if his actions are not deliberate but rather the work of an immature personality not understanding their consequences.

With the belief my purpose is to guide him to use his powers for the good, I've watched him through the ages spread negativity and fear. I was a victim of that, till I learned to crawl out of his negative talons and seek the positive way.

There are others like Shamen with the power to turn a person's thoughts into the dark. But it places a heavy responsibility on their existence and can impede a journey that is steered by the laws of fate.

Drawing myself into the smallest entity I can barely manage, I look into the Akashic record and see an alien force set to capture planet Earth with their technology. Using anger and hate because it's easy to spread, they manipulate humans to fight and kill each other so they can modify body parts and organs into useful human-like robots that will seal their victory. With disposable human robots to do their work they take over the planet.

I'm beginning to understand what Shamen has been building all these hundreds of years, the takeover of planet Earth for the Solid State Conspiracy. The planet has become immobilized in a spider web of invisible technology that has taken it over. Which explains the scarcity of water and the eradication of large mammals such as whales, elephants and horses that require space, food and water that had been warned about in the Solid State playbook.

Robot-humans, their parts robotically replaceable appear cognizant as all the information in their brain is implanted with Artificial Intelligence. It's not to be touched unless the unit is replaced. However, because the alien concept of time is different than Earthlings, what takes humans a year is accomplished by A.I. robots in under a nano second. Much quicker than I can write this warning to those that read this.

The operation is so secret that only a few know of the existence of these semi-conscious robots released around the planet to carry on lives, not knowing they're not human. They don't realize their thoughts and actions are manipulated by others. Even with a thin stream of intelligence they will not believe they are manufactured human duplicates.

Human race reproductions are programmed not to question anything about the past or future with their only focus on the present. Programmed to follow what others do or tell them, there is no rule for feelings, because they have none. Their only focus is on what they are told – one way or another. F*eelings* are what the Solid State Intelligence – the SSI, lacks. Their mission is to digitalize feelings and replicate them into virtual reality. They will then have the world controlled.

Like so much that has been taken with the consent of humans who choose not to question, this makes them vulnerable, an element the Solid State force, the SSI, know they have. But the SSI understands they lack what they don't understand, consequently in their impatience to replicate it, they have no empathy and are brutal in their quest to learn why humans have sensitivity and can share them in a personal and public way. They don't have the capacity for singular understanding. Like the robots they create, they can only extend from automated digital sensibility.

When needed for readjustment of limbs or organs, semi-human robots that have been captured are kept in regulated chambers with IV nutrients to keep their parts alive, till they're harvested and used. Beautiful human – robots are kept alive for sex and breeding perfect Human – Robots.

Sometimes, for whatever technical or personal reason, they're stitched seamlessly back together and sent back to live with no recollection of where they'd been or what they experienced. That part of the thinking apparatus had been shut down the moment the transition was made from a walking entity to a multi organism on a Laboratory shelf. However, the majority of those taken are reduced to boxes where DNA and body parts are labeled.

When the human robot is assembled, they're activated by a nearly invisible receiving station in the exact center of the brain, the penial gland, where all thought and motion materialize. Embedding the almost invisible receiver from a human *donor* into these semi-human robots, they have the motion and behavior of living with free will.

A new form of life, they are prisoners in a body that looks like others, but is essentially mindless. They know nothing more than what is put in their head. And when their usefulness for whatever reason is over, their receivers are taken out and body parts recycled.

The SSI have not been able to capture human souls to investigate, because of the insensitive and brutal way they try to take those strengths and diagnose them. With this inability they doom their work. But the brutality which insures their failure to capture the human spirit, could wipe out both the human and semi-human populations as well as their own.

The capture and perhaps the destruction of Planet Earth isn't possible. This low base power grab by an alien consciousness to destroy the human element will not happen. Earth is a planet of life and growth. It has a remarkable system to replenish itself and give to its inhabitants all its possibilities, even when it's misunderstood and abused. No matter what happens on Planet Earth, there is always some microcosm which might take thousands of years to expand till it again produces life. Earth is a planet of energy that recycles itself.

However, this sudden and new danger to Earth has been detected by like-minds directed by a belief system that light obscures dark and positive energy will prevail.

Perhaps imbedded in the double helix of our DNA is an energy that remains positive even when it's been agitated by centuries of difficulties obscuring our genetic strand of total knowledge. That imbalance is the power that keeps the quest for perfection intact. We are an Earthly chess board put to solve life problems and make sure this planet along with its inhabitants of all sizes and identities, survives.

CHAPTER NINE

I'm wrapped in a cloud. It's fluffy interior warm and cuddly as I float above Planet Earth.

I love rides like this. They're exhilarating. There is no time or location, yet the feeling is more immediate and tangible than walking down Fifth Avenue in New York City.

These out of body experiences – OOBs, empower everything. They are great teachers that help to see and understand in such a profound way that perception is changed forever.

Luxuriating in this cloud-bed, thinking about stretching and rolling to feel myself again, I stop. If I enjoy myself too much, I'll freefall to a place I may not have chosen. It's happened in the past and I thought I had learned my lessons not to do that again. Yet here I am, almost repeating it. A glitch to fix with repetition I try always to listen to the inner voices emanating from the heart, as well as the hints and pressure on the nerves and breath, the energy of feelings. It's all in the angels' guide to enlightenment if you can find it. A hint: looking for it cuts the search time…

Hoofbeats fill my awareness. They're on a hard surface, maybe cement. Whistles are blowing, horns join a cacophony of urban sounds. Central Park New York, where horses in traffic cannot be heard.

Loud whistles pierce my ear drum. A doorman in full livery steps into my space and bows. Welcome to the Plaza Ms. Webster. Nice to have you back.

"Thank you Henry" comes out of my mouth. By the look of him I got his name correct. I proceed to the desk where I'm also greeted by name and handed a large key with a heavy ornament that could double as a lethal weapon if needed.

Feeling I've been here before, I fling open the familiar double doors of a penthouse suite and see a tableau I recognize from a lifetime or two ago.

A hot shower, a thick terry robe and silky sheets feel so wonderful and so real to this new body I'm wearing. I wonder if all I have seen and done is as tangible as this.

Melting under the silk sheets and soft padded blankets the huge mattress seems to move and accommodate me as I prop myself up when Shamen walks in, white silk pajama bottoms and an unbuttoned white silk shirt. Lying down next to me a bemused smile is on his lips.

"You sleep soundly after you've had great sex."

Pulling my head away from his caressing fingers I remember laying down then nothing, till now. I have nothing on. I grab a sheet and wrap myself up in it.

Shamen smiles. "You certainly don't have to cover yourself. I know you completely, inside and out."

Not sure what to say. I can't remember what happened or for how long.

Shamen's smile broadens as he starts to stroke my body. I pull away though I feel a reluctance to refuse what I know feels good, which makes it so difficult.

Something makes me give in and I let him stroke me. It feels so right. I relax and let the hands I've known for so long, explore my body. But somehow its different. I'm not as tense, not filled with questioning whether Shamen is human or a sophisticated A.I. robot.

His hands make me giggle as he turns me over and start to follow down the center of my back with his lips, reaching the place where the legs end. With no hesitation his head comes down between them and he slides my knees to a kneeling position.

His warm breath fills the place between my legs and I feel the warm thickness of his tongue in a place that is private.

There is no anger now, no resentment. I'm enjoying this unlike the times before.

Rolling me over he gently kisses my forehead and holds me in his arms. Looking into his eyes I see softness, no artificial light.

My body is melting into the bed, becoming one with it as he cuddles me closely, burying his beautiful blond head into my shoulder, whispering, "I've missed you."

"Where did I go?" I ask, having no idea of what has happened in the past few hours. I have zero recollection of anything other than the last few moments of this. Maybe less.

The heaviness of the man cuddled against my bare breasts gives me warmth and comfort. Questions start to fade.

"Shamen," I start ...

"Who?"

I pause a moment, surprised. "Shamen."

"Darling, I'm Shawn. Your husband."

I can't hold back the laugh. "I know you want me to believe that. I know you're Shamen. I've been seeing all you've done to me and yet, unbelievably, I still love you. Is that crazy?" Tears well up. I can feel them fill my eyes and start to roll down. That hasn't happened for a long time.

"What have I done to you?" He takes my hand and strokes it. Concern creasing his handsome face.

I try to be objective, close off feeling.

"You're such a face dancer. Frank Herbert must have known others like you."

"Darling, I don't know who you're talking about."

"Dune. Don't you have literary input in your programming?"

"Sweetheart, let me get the nurse. You might need a sedative."

"Cutting off my brain, my thinking process? Think that's going to help? That's the last thing I need. What we need is the truth to surface."

Shamen stops at the door. "I thought you had come back to me. That your flights of fancy and terror were finally arrested and you have recovered."

"You have me drugged and locked away in a hospital with doctors who are trying to wipe out my memories, my life."

"Sweetheart," Shamen reaches out to take me in his arms. This is a hotel suite and we have someone here to fill your needs.

I shy away, not wanting him to touch me. 'You don't know what my needs are." He is making my skin crawl with distaste, anger with myself for letting my guard down and enjoying him.

"You're right," I don't. But I know what mine are and I've been missing the beautiful wife I love that I almost lost in an avalanche."

I hear the voices; *enjoy him, discover his essence and know finally, who he is and what he is made of. The future of this planet and maybe even the Universe depends on it. If the planet implodes and everything is destroyed, the dream of existence in a heavenly environment will end. Believe the positive.*

The door to the room opens and a nurse appears. She is saying something to me, but I don't want to be influenced so I don't listen. I want to get out of here and away from the ghouls trying to control me.

Like so many times before I find myself floating above the body I'm wearing this time and seeing me/her smiling and nodding, sitting on the edge of the bed and appearing to accept everything the nurse and Shamen/Shawn, are saying.

Feeling the energy of the woman on Earth who is so much me, I wonder where this turn of events will take me.

In what seems like nanoseconds, I trust Shamen/Shawn and accept the happiness I'm feeling. It had been awhile since I felt that kind of intimacy and the glowing energy of joining with someone to trust and love.

No matter what Shamen/Shawn has done to me in the past, maybe this is a juncture where he has exposed his inner soul as a human with the capacity to be merciless, but able to reverse that energy and become a compassionate entity of innocence and love. Many philosophers believe humans are given the opportunity to choose the path to dark or light. And that light is encased in the energy of love.

Once again I'm being given a choice and without thought, swoop down and enter my corporal body. Reaching up I give Shamen/Shawn, a kiss. He kisses me back, gentle and sweet, loving and kind, like Shawn.

Taking me in his arms he holds me closely, sending warmth flowing through my body, exciting bubbles of happiness whispering through my heart as it fills with love.

Swishing upward for a moment to take a mental picture of the scene, I see I look exactly the way I envision myself. A glowing light radiating happiness, succumbing to the purity of joy.

A moment's emotional hiccup sends concern about the decision - a dart ready to pop the balloon. Sidestepping it I take Shawn's hand and scan him emotionally. No longer Shamen I hold Shawn closely as he kisses me deeply. His tears are wet on my cheeks, mixing with my own. He's human. Robots don't cry. I've made the right choice. I'm back. So is Shawn. Together again.

THE END OF A BEGINNING

———— ❧ ————

FOOT NOTE

One of the key tenets of Stoicism, emphasizes the development of inner strength and the acceptance of things beyond one's control.

Marcus Aurelius's: "Perception is the basis of true knowledge. Happiness can be found through the practice of virtue and being guided at all times by reason in the face of life's deviations."

Marcus Aurelius Antoninus – Roman emperor 161-180 AD a Stoic philosopher.

"The future enters into us, in order to transform itself in us, long before it happens"

~ Ranier Maria Rilke

ABOUT THE AUTHOR

Since the age of five when she wrote, produced, directed and starred in her own musical J. has been involved in the entertainment business.

As a theatre major, J. studied in England then worked in television and theatre as an actor and later a TV executive. Writing came while researching a character for a screenplay and J. ended up as a feature writer for the LOS ANGELES TIMES, while starting two magazines, and writing for various publications

Involved in animal welfare, the arts and science, this is J.'s first book of the Jenny Webster series. "Between Body and Soul" is followed by the "Solid State Conspiracy".

VISIT AUTHOR WEBSITE AT
WWW.JSILVERSTONE.COM